The rumors are flying
behind closed doors. . . .

"Who? Kayla? What makes you think that?"

Hearing my own name made my heart pound. I held my breath and listened.

"Shhh! Lots of things. Number one: her clothes. Everything she wears is . . ."

There were voices, several voices. I couldn't tell how many. Two, three, maybe even more than that. But they were whispering, so it was hard for me to recognize them.

". . . isn't it weird about all that mail and . . ."

". . . some special reason to make phone calls . . ."

"Yeah, and where is she really from? I mean, she obviously isn't . . ."

I was pressing my ear against the crack of the door, straining to hear.

Who was it? Boo? Shelby? Betsy? I just couldn't tell.

I pictured all seven of the Cabin 4 girls standing around washing their hands. Talking, talking, talking. About me.

One Summer. One Sleepaway Camp.
Three Thrilling Stories!

How far will Kelly
go to hold on to
her new friends?

What happens when Judith
Ducksworth decides to
become JD at camp?

Can Darcy and
Nicole's friendship
survive the summer?

Summer Camp Secrets

RUMORS

by
Katy Grant

ALADDIN
New York London Toronto Sydney

To my "gold" friends I thought I had lost
but have found once more

ALADDIN
An imprint of Simon & Schuster Children's Publishing Division
1230 Avenue of the Americas, New York, NY 10020
First Aladdin paperback edition May 2010
Text copyright © 2010 by Katy Grant
All rights reserved, including the right of reproduction in whole or in part in any form.
ALADDIN is a trademark of Simon & Schuster, Inc., and related logo is a registered trademark of Simon & Schuster, Inc.
For information about special discounts for bulk purchases, please contact Simon & Schuster Special Sales at 1-866-506-1949 or business@simonandschuster.com.
The Simon & Schuster Speakers Bureau can bring authors to your live event. For more information or to book an event contact the Simon & Schuster Speakers Bureau at 1-866-248-3049 or visit our website at www.simonspeakers.com.
Designed by Karin Paprocki
The text of this book was set in Perpetua.
Manufactured in the United States of America 0310 OFF
10 9 8 7 6 5 4 3 2 1
Library of Congress Control Number 2010922217
ISBN 978-1-4169-9163-2
ISBN 978-1-4424-0668-1 eBook

Acknowledgments

I want to first thank my wonderful friend Amy Lerman, who helped me with the piano-playing scenes. I can play the right-hand part of "Heart and Soul" on the piano, and a little bit of "Chopsticks," but that is about the extent of my repertoire. So Amy met me for lunch (we both love having an excuse to meet), answered all of my questions, and gave me numerous suggestions. Then she was happy to read over the chapters that featured Kayla playing the piano and patiently endured yet another round of my questions. I love having talented friends I can call on to help me with subjects I know little to nothing about!

And now a note about the dedication. I didn't move a lot growing up, but I did move twice during my school years and attended college out of state. I then moved to Arizona, where I have lived for the past twenty-plus years, far away from my Tennessee roots. When I lost touch with old friends, I didn't give it much thought. I had made new friends, and I was too busy living in the present to think much about my past.

But this year, 2009, has been a year of reunions and reconnections for me. Through the wonders of the Internet, I have found many old friends I thought

I had lost forever. Reconnecting with one friend led to another and another and another. I now am in touch with dozens of junior high school friends, high school friends, and camp friends whom I had not seen or spoken to in almost thirty years. I have come to realize that true friendships are never really lost, no matter how many years pass. So this book is for all those long-lost, rediscovered friends I cherish more now than ever. You truly are golden.

CHAPTER 1

Sunday, June 15

At least this was only temporary. I was stuck here at this summer camp for four weeks, and then we would move to the new house. I could put up with just about anything for four weeks.

It could be worse. I could have a horrible earache right now. It could be raining. I could be stuck at math camp instead of just plain old summer camp. A math camp where they only served lima beans for dinner every day. So this was better than being stuck at math camp with an earache while eating lima beans in the middle of a rainstorm. That cheered me up just a little bit.

As I looked around, I realized I was the only person standing still while all around me, everyone was moving. Climbing up and down the big hill in front of us. Waving to someone in the crowd. Asking questions or giving directions. Carrying suitcases, pillows, sleeping bags.

A car pulled up, and even before it came to a stop, a girl with long brown hair threw open the back door and jumped out. Two other girls ran up and hugged her. "What cabin are you in? Which counselor did we get?" At least some people were happy to be here.

A long line of cars was slowly creeping up the gravel road, and I watched scenes like this over and over. Sometimes the girl in the car got out slowly and looked around. No one ran up to her car and screamed and hugged her, so I could tell she was a new girl, like me. Her parents would stand there for a few seconds looking confused, until one of the counselors in the green shirts would say hello and give them instructions about what to do and where to go.

It reminded me of the time our family was in New York City on vacation, and we went to Grand Central Station and watched all the people coming and going in the big lobby.

But this was North Carolina, not New York. And we weren't in the city anymore, that was for sure. I couldn't believe all the nature I was seeing for the first time. Mama and Daddy put Samantha and me on the plane this morning, and as we were coming in for the landing, all I could see were green mountains, trees, and rivers everywhere.

Nearby the camp director and a big group of counselors were busy welcoming parents and girls. A counselor in a green shirt noticed I was by myself and walked up to me. "Hey! Can I help you find anything?"

"Oh, no thanks. I told my little sister to meet me here after she moved into her cabin."

We were standing under shade trees in front of the dining hall. Behind us was a wooden footbridge across a stream, and hidden behind some trees was a little cabin that looked like it came right out of pioneer times, with a couple of rocking chairs on the porch and flowered curtains hanging in the open windows.

She glanced at the wooden name tag I was wearing around my neck. "Well, Kayla, it's nice to meet you. I'm Libby. If you have any questions, just let me or one of the other counselors know, okay?"

"Thanks. Actually . . . is there a piano somewhere that I could practice on a little sometimes?"

"Oh, yeah. There's a piano in each of the lodges. You can go in there any time during free time and practice."

"Thanks! Nice to meet you, Libby," I said.

She walked off to talk to some other people. Then I noticed Samantha far away at the top of the hill, and when she saw me waving, she started running in my direction. The dozens of beaded braids in her hair were all bouncing as she ran. I'd worn my hair like that when I was younger, but I'd gotten a short haircut for the summer.

Three other girls were running with Samantha. By the time they got to me, they were all out of breath. "This place is so cool!" Samantha announced.

I couldn't keep from smiling. "You like it?"

"I don't like it. I love it! And these are my friends. We're all in the same cabin. Junior Cabin Two. Gracie, Mary Claire, and Alyssa—meet my sister Kayla. She's twelve. That makes her a Middler." We'd just found out that there were three different age groups here at Pine Haven.

Alyssa, the one with big teeth and long, dark hair hanging in her eyes, looked me up and down. "Huh. You look older than twelve."

"Well, I'll be thirteen in September," I told her. "Did you get your sheets unpacked and your bed made?" I asked Samantha.

She nodded. "I picked out a top bunk. And I thought there weren't any bathrooms, but there are. Only they're not inside the cabins. There's this other building with faucets on one side and bathroom stalls on the other."

"We found out the name for the bathrooms is 'Solitary.' Isn't that weird?" asked Gracie, the smallest girl, with bright red hair. She was holding Samantha's hand.

"And we're the first ones to get moved into our cabin. Every cabin has eight girls and two counselors. So four more girls aren't even here yet. But the four of us are already friends, and we just met ten minutes ago!"

Samantha was so excited she bounced up and down on her toes. I was glad she was fitting right in, but there was something I wanted to warn her about.

"Can I talk to you for one second?" I reached for her arm and led her down the path a little ways.

"Now what?" she groaned. "My friends are waiting for me."

I sighed. "I want you to have fun here and everything, but remember one thing, okay? We're only at Camp Pine Haven for a short time. Then we move to the new house."

It wasn't the first time we'd moved, and it probably wouldn't be the last. I just didn't want Samantha getting all attached to these girls she might never see again.

Samantha's mouth opened in amazement, and her forehead wrinkled up. "What do you mean, a short time? We're here for a whole month!"

"I know. A month sounds like a long time, but it'll go by fast," I warned her. I wanted to remind her that practically as soon as she made these friends, she'd be saying good-bye to them and starting all over again.

"I'm glad you're meeting some other girls, but . . ."

"But what?" She glared at me with her dark brown eyes.

What was I supposed to tell her? Don't bother to make friends because we're just passing through? You think these girls are your new best friends, but next year you might not even remember what they look like?

"But don't forget that I'm your sister, and I'm your real best friend," I said finally. I tried to hug her, but she slipped out of my arms and danced backward a few steps.

"Okay. Whatever!" she said, shaking her head and making her braids bounce. She didn't like it when I got too affectionate with her.

She ran back to Gracie and grabbed her hand. "Come on. Let's go explore the rest of the camp." And she was off with her new friends without looking back.

I just hoped she wouldn't be too upset when camp

was over. Friends come and go, but family is forever. That was one thing I'd learned from all the times we'd had to move. Maybe Samantha would learn that lesson soon. The sooner she figured that out, the better off she'd be.

I hadn't met one single person yet, and I was fine with that. It wouldn't be hard to go without friends for a month. I could put up with just about anything for a month.

Except maybe an earache and lima beans.

CHAPTER 2

"Since you're new, we'll be happy to help you out. After lights out, it's okay for us to talk to each other as late as we want," said Boo Bauer.

She was a heavyset girl with blond hair and big round glasses that made her eyes look gigantic. She was sitting on the counselor's bed, telling her all kinds of things about the rules. Our counselor's name was Gloria Mendoza, and at lunch she'd told us it was her first year here at Pine Haven. As soon as she'd said that, Boo had pounced on her like a cat chasing a windup mouse.

"During rest hour, campers don't have to sit on their bunks and be quiet. It's totally fine for us to talk or play cards. Oh, and when counselors go on leave, they're supposed to bring candy back to their campers. It's a custom we have around here."

Gloria just smiled at Boo. "Thanks for the help. I think I know the rules, though." She seemed nice. She had a sweet smile and pretty green eyes, and she'd told us her activity was crafts. Every counselor worked at one particular activity.

"I'm an old camper too," said Laurel-Ann Humphreys, the girl with braces and her hair in two braids. "You can always ask me if you have any questions. It's hard being new. I know because I remember what it was like last year. There are all kinds of Pine Haven words you need to know, and lots of traditions. And songs. We sing lots of songs. I think that's the worst part about being new—not knowing all the words to the songs, and you're looking around, and—"

"Hyphen, remember sometimes you need to stop talking and take a breath," Boo told her. "Otherwise you'll pass out." Laurel-Ann frowned at her and went back to unpacking her trunk.

I'd figured out that Hyphen was Laurel-Ann's nickname because her name had a hyphen in it on her name tag. I had no idea what Boo's real name was, if she even had one. I felt awkward saying her name out loud, like I was trying to sneak up on her and scare her.

"I'll take this empty top bunk, if that's okay with everybody," offered Shelby Parsons. She was new like me and thin as a rail.

"Good, I hate the top bunk," said Boo. "You will too when you have to climb down and go to Solitary in the middle of the night."

The four of us were the Side B girls. The other half of the cabin was for the Side A girls and their counselor. We could hear them over there talking and unpacking too, but a low wooden wall separated the cabin into two open rooms.

I was totally okay with that. Meeting three other girls and my new counselor was about all I could handle at the moment.

It was early in the evening, and we'd spent the afternoon at the lake taking swim tests. But now everyone was in the cabin, unpacking, talking, and getting to know each other.

That is, *they* were talking and getting to know each other. I was just unpacking. They could talk as much as they wanted, as long as they left me alone.

I'd taken the bottom bunk under Shelby, and there was a long shelf beside my bed made out of plain, rough wood for me to put my personal items on. I pulled a plastic bag out of my trunk and took out my shampoo, conditioner, toothpaste, and deodorant and lined them all up in a neat row.

These cabins were simple, to say the least. That little cabin near the dining hall with the rocking chairs on the porch had looked cozy, but the cabins where all the campers slept weren't much.

I looked at the bare wooden walls. The cabins wouldn't have looked too bad, except for one thing. People had been signing their names all over, everywhere. I mean, *everywhere*. On the walls, on the wooden boards of the ceiling, on the beams overhead, on the shelves. Some people had even signed the window screens that covered the top part of the front and back walls.

In big black letters. In big white letters. I could hardly see an inch of bare wall that didn't have a name on it somewhere. And the dates—I couldn't believe how old they were! HOLT & BOBO 1974. Now that was old. I glanced around at the ceiling and wondered if this whole cabin would topple over at any minute. You just never knew.

"Why don't you put your pillow down on that end?" Boo told Laurel-Ann. They both had single cots next to each other.

"Why? What does it matter?" asked Laurel-Ann, pulling a purple blanket out of her trunk.

"Because I put my pillow at the other end, and that way, our cots will be head to toe instead of head to head. I don't want to smell your breath all night. Plus, you're less likely to try to carry on a conversation with my feet."

"Well, okay, but it's going to feel weird for me to sleep with my head pointing out toward the middle of the cabin," Laurel-Ann started off, and then she went on and on about what direction her bed at home faced.

I really wished I could stick some cotton balls in my ears so I wouldn't have to listen to everyone.

It was a waste for me to even be here. Instead of unpacking my trunk here, I could be at our old house right now. Even though movers were coming soon to load up the moving van, there was still so much work to do. Mama and Daddy were busy packing boxes and sorting through closets and drawers for things to keep or give away. I could be helping with all that.

I took out a stack of pink towels and put them on one end of my shelf. Then I pulled out a box of blank note cards. I'd promised my friends I'd write them, but I wasn't sure how good I would be about keeping that promise. Next I unpacked a few framed photos I'd brought along of my family. Just looking at my parents' smiling faces made me miss them.

This was our third move, and Samantha and I had always been around to help out with everything. But this time was going to be different. "A real headache," Daddy had called it. We had to be moved out of our old house by a certain date, but we couldn't move into our new house for another twelve days. So that meant twelve days of being stuck in the middle, between two different houses in two different states.

Plus there was the really long drive from Baltimore to Tampa. Then they'd be staying in a hotel for almost two weeks. They just didn't want to put us through all that. So off we went to Pine Haven instead.

I was kneeling in front of my open trunk, sorting through my clothes. I pulled out four new pairs of shorts and tugged on the plastic strings of the price tags until they snapped. Then I did the same thing with the tags on my new shirts. Some of them still had those little size stickers stuck to them. By the time I was finished, there was a small pile of trash on the floor. I scooped it up and carried it to the trash can.

"Wow. All new clothes. I've never seen anyone bring all new clothes to camp before," said Boo. I turned around and saw that she was staring into my open trunk.

I didn't know what I was supposed to say to that, so

I didn't say anything. Now Laurel-Ann and Shelby had stopped what they were doing to watch me too.

What did they care if I brought new clothes, old clothes, or plastic trash bags to wear? If I wanted to wear a grass skirt and dance a hula with a pineapple on top of my head, was it any of their business?

"Are you rich or something?" asked Boo from where she sat on her cot, staring at me with her magnified eyes.

What kind of question was that to ask someone?

"No."

"You got some nice clothes. All designer brands, too," she went on. Shelby and Laurel-Ann couldn't take their eyes off us either.

"Thank you," I said. What else was I supposed to say?

It just so happened that I didn't have a lot of regular clothes, since I had to wear a uniform at my old school. And when I'd started packing for camp, I realized that none of my clothes from last summer fit me anymore. I grew three inches this year.

So Mama had taken Samantha and me on this crazy, last-minute shopping trip yesterday afternoon. I was lucky I had any clothes at all to wear. I easily could've showed up with nothing to wear but some plastic trash bags. Either that or a couple of plaid jumpers and white shirts. I hoped the girls in Samantha's cabin weren't giving her a hard time right now over her new wardrobe.

"Is that your mom? Oh my gosh, she is so pretty!" Laurel-Ann exclaimed. She was leaning down and staring at the pictures on my shelf.

I wondered what else these girls were going to do to invade my privacy. Maybe Shelby would ask me what color undies I'd brought along.

"Yes, that's my mom," I said.

Laurel-Ann picked up the photo of Mama and stood there breathing on it. Could she even see the picture anymore through the fog she was leaving on the glass? "She looks like a movie star! Is she a model or something?"

"No."

That photo was one of Mama's professional head shots, and it wasn't an exaggeration—she did look like a model in it. Her curly black hair had been perfectly styled, and she had on silver loop earrings and a silver necklace that sparkled in the light. The rose-colored eye shadow and lipstick looked fabulous against her smooth brown complexion. It was my favorite picture of her.

"She could be a model, though. What does she do?" asked Laurel-Ann, handing my picture over to Boo so she could give it her own detailed inspection.

"She works at a TV station," I said. I clasped both hands behind my back, because that was the only way I could keep from snatching my picture back and rubbing it down with a towel to get all their fingerprints and foggy breath off it.

"Really?" Boo's jaw practically dropped to the floor. "Doing what?"

"It's kind of hard to explain," I said.

Actually, it wasn't hard to explain at all. All of her jobs have been in broadcast journalism, so basically she did the news. On TV. She'd started off as a feature reporter in the beginning, but her new job was going to be weekend anchor. So it was kind of a big deal. This move was really great for her career.

Boo was staring at me. "What's so hard to explain? Is she on TV or not?"

Should I just tell them? It would sound like I was bragging. *Oh, my mom's on television.* I glanced at Gloria, hoping she'd tell them to mind their own business.

"Why don't you give Kayla the picture back?" she suggested. Three sets of eyes watched me as I casually put it back on the shelf. I'd wipe their fingerprints off later.

It could be worse. I could've ended up with a top bunk like Shelby. Boo could be identical twins. Laurel-

Ann could've dropped Mama's picture and broken the glass. And I might've cut my hand, and then maybe I would get an infection. At least I wasn't sleeping in a top bunk with an infected cut while two identical Boos asked me twice as many questions every time I had to climb down to go to a bathroom called Solitary.

Thinking about that cheered me up a little.

But not much.

CHAPTER 3

The one good thing was that we didn't have lima beans for dinner. We had chicken, green beans, and mashed potatoes. I got to wave to Samantha from across the dining hall, but that was about it. From our table, I could see her talking nonstop to all her new friends. I was glad she was happy, at least. It didn't matter so much about me.

"Good. At least there are vegetarian alternatives," announced Devon Fairchild, one of the Side A girls. She'd gone to the salad bar and gotten a serving of spinach quiche and salad.

Devon had black hair and blue eyes, and her complexion was the same color as a glass of milk. Even though she was a new girl, she seemed to be good friends with Christina Ramirez, a girl with dark, wavy hair and two different colored sneakers on——one yellow, one red.

Maggie Windsor was another friend of Christina's. She had curly red hair, and she told jokes all through dinner. Chris laughed at all of them, but Devon didn't even crack a smile. As far as I could tell, Devon and Maggie had just met each other for the first time, and neither one of them was too happy about that.

The other counselor in our cabin was named Caroline Heyward, but her name tag said WAYWARD on it. She was looking around at all of us and nodding. "Looks like a good cabin. Very Zen."

This Wayward person was kind of strange. All day she'd walked around in sunglasses and a pink and gray plaid hat. I'd heard her tell a couple of parents that she was a riding counselor and that she'd been coming to Pine Haven for fourteen years.

That was a big topic of discussion around here—— how many years you'd been coming to this camp. The longer, the better, it seemed like. But I doubted I'd ever stay in one place for fourteen years.

After dinner, I tried to squeeze through the crowd so I could talk to Samantha for a second, but there were too many people in the way, so I couldn't get to her.

Outside, the sun had slipped down behind the mountains that were way off in the distance. The light was all soft now, and I couldn't get over how green everything was. I'd never seen this many trees before in my life.

I was walking up the big hill toward our cabin when Betsy Smith, the Side A girl with short blond hair, came up to me. She'd been in my group during the swim tests, but other than that, I hadn't talked to her much.

"The first day is kind of weird, isn't it? Is this your first year?" Betsy asked.

"Uh-huh. How about you?"

"Yeah, it's my first year, but my mother came here, so I've been hearing Pine Haven stories forever. I was destined to come here eventually."

All of a sudden, a feeling of sadness pressed down on me. People who came back year after year after year. Girls who had mothers who came here. It was like they all belonged. Even the new girls already had ties to this place. And I'd probably leave here in a month and never come back.

Oh, well. It didn't matter.

I tried to think of something to say to Betsy, but there was a long pause. Luckily, Laurel-Ann came panting up beside us.

"All these hills! My legs are hurting already. But

don't worry. You'll get used to it. Now we go to evening program. In the lodge. I'll show y'all where it is. We should all sit together. I was a newbie last year, and I didn't have any friends at first. Now I've got lots of friends here, but you can always make more, right?"

And from that point on, I didn't need to worry anymore about making conversation, because Laurel-Ann had taken over.

I was anxious to see the lodge, because I wanted to check out the piano. When we filed through the large wooden doors, I immediately spotted it pushed up against one wall. There were two girls sitting on the bench with their backs to the piano and their elbows resting on the keyboard. I wouldn't even have a chance to go over and strike a few keys to hear its tone.

The noise was deafening in here with all the people inside. This lodge was huge—one big room with stone walls and an arched ceiling overhead. There was a fireplace on one wall, and through the back door I could see people sitting out on a porch.

Laurel-Ann, Betsy, and I found an empty spot on the floor and sat down cross-legged.

"Are the Juniors coming to this too?" I asked Laurel-Ann.

"Oh, no. This is just the Middler evening program.

The Juniors and Seniors are in their own lodges right now."

This camp seemed determined to keep Samantha and me separated.

After a few minutes, all the counselors came in and announced that we'd be doing get-acquainted games.

"Okay, the first game we're going to play is 'Where Are You From?'" called out Libby, the counselor I'd met earlier. "Look around and you'll see counselors holding signs with names of different states. If you don't see your state—and we didn't make fifty signs—Jamie, our riflery counselor, is holding a blue sign that says, 'Elsewhere.'"

Everyone laughed at that. "Okay. Go find the other girls from your state!"

We all stood up and started moving around the room. There was a sign for Maryland, but only a couple of girls were standing in that group. I looked around until I saw the Florida sign. That group was bigger, with about six or seven girls in it.

So which sign should I stand under? I started moving toward the Maryland sign, but then I felt a sudden pain in my heart. As of today, I didn't live in Maryland anymore.

I glanced over at the Florida group. But I hadn't actually lived there yet. I didn't belong there, either.

Too bad those groups weren't side by side. Maybe I could stand with one foot in each one. Or should I head for the "Elsewhere" group? That's where it felt like I was from at the moment.

I turned around and was suddenly face-to-face with Shelby. "Oh, hey! Are you from Tennessee?" she asked.

I don't know what made me do it, but I did. "It looks like it," I said. What difference did it make? This was a big group, and I guess I thought I could blend in.

But that didn't happen. I soon found out what a big mistake it was to make a detour through Tennessee when you're not really from there.

One girl was walking around asking everyone, "East, Middle, or West?"

I had no idea what that was all about, so when the girl next to me said middle, I said East. Then the girl with the geography obsession started asking everyone which city they were from.

By now I was feeling totally panicked. My heart was beating so fast, I couldn't even think straight. I had to get out of there. I glanced around the crowded room and noticed that the windows were open. Would they be surprised if I suddenly jumped through one?

"Where are you from?" Geography Girl asked me.

I'd heard a few people name off towns I'd never heard of. I could try that.

"Oh, it's a really small town. You've probably never heard of it," I said.

"Well, what city's it near?" she asked.

Cities in Tennessee. I'd heard people say Chatta-nooga, Knoxville, Nashville. Suddenly an old song popped into my head that my father would sometimes sing about trying to place a call to . . . "Memphis, Ten-nessee," I blurted out.

Geography Girl was about to pass me by and ask the next person, when she stopped and gave me a strange look. "Hang on. I thought you said you were from East Tennessee a second ago. And you live near Memphis?" Geography Girl made a face. "You can't live near Mem-phis. That's in West Tennessee!"

It was like everyone in this big group had suddenly decided we should switch from a geography bee to a game of freeze tag. They all stopped dead still. And everyone was staring. Right at me.

If Geography Girl had had a spotlight, she would've turned it on me at that moment. Was it too late to jump out that window?

"Uh," I answered. What could I say? It was such a stu-pid thing to lie about. Why did I pick a state I'd never lived in? I had three different states to choose from, so what was I thinking?

All these eyes were on me. I've never been a mind reader before, but looking around at everyone, I could read every single mind in this group. And they were all saying the same thing: *You're so full of it.*

"Yeah, you don't sound like you're from Tennessee. Where are you really from?" another girl asked. Shelby was standing beside her. She looked like she felt sorry for me, but she didn't say anything. I couldn't really blame her.

"Baltimore. In Maryland. But we're moving this week," I said finally. I didn't dare say we were moving to Tennessee. One lie would just lead to another.

At that moment the counselors announced the next game. "Okay, now we want to know what your sign is! Find your zodiac sign and get with your group!"

I heard someone behind me whisper, "She doesn't know where she lives. You think she knows when her birthday is?"

And then laughter.

My whole face was burning with embarrassment.

Up until now, the most embarrassing moment of my life was the time I tied my shoelaces together during story time in first grade, and then I couldn't get them untied. When it was time to go to lunch, I couldn't even walk. I had cried, and everyone had laughed, and my teacher, Mrs. Schubert, couldn't get them unknotted, so she had to cut them with her scissors.

That was horrible.

But this was worse.

We kept playing these games for the rest of the evening. We had to get in groups by birth order—oldest, youngest, middle, or only child—and by hair color. Every time I was in a group with one of the Tennessee girls, I gave that open window another consideration.

Finally the games were over. We all had to get into a big circle and sing "Taps," and then they gave us graham crackers and milk. After that, we were supposed to go to our cabins and get ready for bed.

I was one of the first out the door. I dashed to the cabin and flipped on the light switch to get my toothpaste and toothbrush. But by the time I got to the bathrooms, it was already getting crowded in there.

When I got back to the cabin, just about everyone was changing into pajamas. As soon as Boo saw me, she said, "Oh, hi, Kayla! Where'd you say you were from again?" She said it in a really friendly voice, but there was something about her tone that made me nervous.

Had Shelby told them? She wasn't even in here

at the moment. I passed her going to the bathrooms when I was coming back. But Boo must have heard somehow.

I wished there was a way you could not answer a question without being rude. "I've lived in a few different states," I said finally.

"Really? Like where?" Boo asked. She was sitting on her cot with her legs crossed. Without her glasses on, her eyes didn't look so big, but they still had a way of staring right through you.

"Well, I was born in Illinois," I said. That seemed like a safe answer. Why would anyone say they were from one state when they weren't? Should I even try to explain it?

"Illinois? That's not what I heard!" And then Boo started laughing. I could feel myself blushing all over again. Even though I'd just come from the bathrooms, I grabbed a washcloth and a bar of soap and scooted out of the cabin as fast as I could.

My face felt so hot, I figured I'd better wash it before it caught on fire. What would people think if I walked around with this washcloth draped over my face for the next four weeks?

After I'd washed my face, I hid in one of the stalls. Eventually I heard a counselor outside yell, "Lights

' So I came out of the bathroom and got back to the
~~bin~~ as fast as I could.

There was a good thing and a bad thing about going
back to the cabin in the dark. The good thing was
nobody could see me. The bad thing was I couldn't see
a foot in front of me. I stumbled against something that
felt like a stack of bricks, and I had to bite my lip to
keep from yelling.

"Kayla, is that you?" I heard Gloria's voice through
the darkness. "Need me to turn on the light?"

"No! That's okay! I can see just fine," I told her.

"Yeah, that's right," Boo called out, really loudly. "It's
a little-known fact that all people from Tennessee have
X-ray vision. Right, Kayla?" And then I could hear her
laughing.

I crawled into my bed. I was pretty sure it was my
bed. Luckily, no one else was in it, so I decided it must
be mine.

I rubbed my bruised shins and pulled the covers up
around me.

What a horrible first day.

It could've been worse, though. I could've failed
the swim test this afternoon like one girl did. She had
to be rescued by a counselor. Or right in the middle
of the states game, I could've jumped out that window.

But I probably would've ended up with a broken ankle or something. And then the counselors would've had to carry me away on a stretcher while all the other girls stood around talking about how I couldn't swim, I'd never make it as a stuntwoman, and I didn't even know what state I was from.

Now that the lights were out and everyone was quiet, I heard something. Lots and lots of sounds coming from outside. It sort of sounded like a jungle out there. I lay in bed, trying to figure out what kinds of wild creatures were making all those noises.

Crickets, definitely. But there were some other loud sounds. *Burap, burap, burap, burap.* What on earth was that? And why wasn't everyone else sitting up and commenting about how noisy it was outside? After about five minutes of listening, I figured out that maybe it was frogs making that sound. The next thing I noticed was cows mooing. Was I ever going to fall asleep?

It seemed like half an hour passed with me just lying there, listening to all the crazy noises. About that time, I heard another sound I could easily identify.

The sound of somebody crying.

And I could tell where it was coming from: Shelby's bunk right above me.

I guess I wasn't the only one who had a bad day.

CHAPTER 4

Monday, June 16

"Hi! You're Kayla Tucker, right?" asked Eda Thompson, the camp director, when I came through the screen door.

"Yes. I'm supposed to get a phone call today from my parents," I reminded her.

"That's fine, Kayla. You can have a seat there," she said, pointing to a chair by the wall. She went into another room, and I sat down to wait.

This was the first time I'd been inside the camp office. It had the same form of air-conditioning that every other building in camp had—window screens— but there was also a ceiling fan whirring overhead. In front of me was a desk, and a clock was ticking on the wall.

We'd just finished lunch, and I'd discovered my new favorite thing about Pine Haven: We got to check our mailboxes after lunch every day. There were rows of little cubbyholes on the dining hall porch, each with a name taped above it. And today, in my box, I'd had an amazing surprise. There were postcards inside it. Nine postcards! My friends had all written me already.

I sat in the chair and looked through all the pictures. There was one with the Hollywood sign, another from Universal Studios, one with a California beach scene, a couple with pictures of old movie stars. I loved all the variety, and I wondered if my friends had made a point of each buying different cards to send me.

My school orchestra was in Los Angeles right now on a trip. A fantastic trip that I would've been on too. If we weren't moving.

I couldn't believe they'd all written me—Danielle had to be behind this. She was my best friend, and she was very good at organizing things. She'd even gotten Brian to write me a postcard. He was sort of my boyfriend.

Just then the phone rang, and I jumped a little. Eda came out of the room she was in to answer it. "I wonder who that could be?" she asked me with a wink. "Camp Pine Haven for Girls. This is Eda," she said into the receiver.

I stood up, shuffling all my postcards together in a pile. "Why yes, she's right here," she said, smiling and holding the phone out for me. Then she disappeared again.

"Hello?"

"Hi, cutie! How are you?" Mama's warm voice poured through the receiver and wrapped around me like a hug.

"Fine, Mama! Everything's going really well so far!" I said, trying to make my voice sound happy. I told her all about the flight yesterday, and how excited Samantha was about the camp.

Then I asked about how the move was going. The movers were coming in two days, so it sounded like things were super busy. Mama let me talk to Daddy for a few minutes, and then she got back on again.

"Well, don't worry about us," I told her. "This camp was a good idea. I don't get to spend a lot of time with Samantha, but I did see her in between activities this morning. She'd been to canoeing and the climbing tower, and she loved them. And it seems like she's made about fifteen or twenty new friends already."

"Well, that's wonderful. I'm glad to hear all about

how your sister's doing. But now I want to hear about you. How's my big girl?"

That was when my throat closed up and my eyes started to sting. All of a sudden, I felt like crying. I had to take a deep breath to keep myself under control.

"Kayla, cutie? Are you okay?"

"Oh, I'm great! I went to tennis this morning, and archery. And the girls here are so nice, Mama. There's Laurel-Ann, and Shelby, and Chris, and Maggie."

"Well, I'm glad to hear it. But honey, remember what I told you. It's okay to be sad about leaving all your friends and—"

"Oh, Mama! I'm sorry—I have to get off now. The bell just rang and we're about to start a new activity. Are you going to call again on Saturday?" I asked. I hoped Eda hadn't heard me from the other room, making up stuff to my own mother.

"Yes, I'll call Saturday morning at ten o'clock. How's that?"

"Perfect! Love you. Love Daddy. Bye!"

I hung up the phone and sat there until I was sure that I could control myself. There was a box of Kleenex on the desk, so I took one and dabbed at my eyes. I hated rushing through our phone call. But there were some things we just didn't need to talk about.

When I stepped outside, bright sunlight blinded me for a couple of seconds. The whole camp looked empty now because it was rest hour, and everyone was in the cabins. And since I was already late, I hurried up the hill to the row of cabins that was called Middler Line.

Cabin 4 was really quiet when I walked in. Everyone was on her own bunk, reading or writing letters, and on Side A, Wayward was sound asleep on her cot.

The second I came through the door, Boo snapped at me, "Where've you been? You're late!"

I just shrugged a little before going to my bunk. The last thing I wanted to do right now was draw attention to myself.

"Hey, what's the deal? Kayla comes in late for rest hour, and everybody's fine with that? Don't you even want to know where she's been?" Boo was looking back and forth between me and Gloria.

"Shh," Gloria said softly. "It's okay. She was in the office making a phone call."

That made Boo sit up in her bed and stare at me. "A phone call? How come she gets to make a phone call? I thought campers weren't allowed to use the phone, ever."

I tried to keep from groaning out loud. Why did Gloria have to say that?

"Boo, never mind, okay? Kayla has some special

circumstances," Gloria told her. I could feel my cheeks getting warm. At least Gloria hadn't gone into a really long explanation about the fact that I couldn't write letters to my parents like everyone else because there wasn't any place for me to mail them to at this point. What address should I use? Mr. and Mrs. Joseph Tucker, Somewhere between MD and FL, ZIP code: Your guess is as good as mine?

At least getting these postcards had cheered me up, and I still had all of them to read. I spread them out on my blanket with the picture sides up, and now I turned them over one at a time. The first one I read was from my friend Maricela. It was short and sweet, telling me how the string section just didn't sound the same without me on the viola, but they were still having a great time in L.A. Then I read cards from Emily, Megan, Elizabeth, Nadeem, Taylor, David, and Brian.

Brian did say he missed me, and that made me smile. But in some ways, knowing that Brian did like me made me feel worse. Just when I was getting my first boyfriend, we had to move. Maybe Brian would find a new girlfriend this year. Or maybe he wouldn't. Either way, there was one thing I knew for sure.

I'd never be his girlfriend now that I was moving away.

I had saved Danielle's postcard to read last, so now I turned that one over.

Kayla,

I can't even believe that you're not here on this trip with us. You should be here!! It's so messed up that you had to move. I HATE IT!! I MISS YOU SO MUCH!!!! Call me the SECOND you escape from that camp so we can plan a visit. I'm going to make my parents let me come to Florida to visit you before school starts. Write me back as soon as you get this!!

Love ya,

Danielle

I gathered up all the postcards and got up to put them away in my trunk. Then I lay down on my bunk and stared at the metal springs of Shelby's bed above me. It was really nice of my friends to write me. To let me know they missed me and were thinking about me. But I just felt so sad all of a sudden.

There they all were, in Los Angeles, having so much fun with the orchestra. But I wasn't with them. I wasn't a part of that group anymore, and I'd never be a part of it again. I didn't belong.

I just wished I could talk to Danielle right now. Maybe I could write her and then mail her letter tomorrow. It would be there waiting for her when she got home from the L.A. trip.

I reached for the box of blank note cards on the shelf beside my bed and took one out. Then I grabbed a pen. But as I stared at the whiteness of the page in front of me, I couldn't think of anything to say.

I knew Danielle and I would try to keep in touch, but I also knew how these things went. The last time we'd moved was between fourth and fifth grades. My best friend in fourth grade was Leslie Shillingburg. I couldn't even remember the last time I'd heard from her. It seemed like forever. And yet we'd been best friends too, just like Danielle and I were now.

I put the note cards back on my shelf. Maybe I could write her later when I was in a better mood.

Rest hour ended when we heard someone ringing the big bell on the dining hall porch.

Shelby climbed down from her top bunk and put away the Batman comic book she'd been reading. Even though I suspected she'd told everyone about how stupid I looked during the states game last night, I still felt sorry for her after hearing her cry last night. She was obviously homesick, but at least she seemed okay now.

Boo stood up and tugged on her blond ponytail while staring at me with her big glassy eyes. "Where'd all those postcards come from?" she asked me.

I swear, I'd never met anyone as blunt as this girl.

"From my mailbox," I answered. I knew it sounded snotty and mean, but I couldn't help it. Why wouldn't she leave me alone?

"You got mail? Already? We just got here yesterday, and you already got a stack of mail? Plus you get to use the phone whenever you feel like it. Aren't you special!"

Laurel-Ann was pulling on her sneakers. "I love getting mail. I didn't get any today, though. My parents said they'd write me this week, and my sister, and my grandma's going to write too."

"Maybe you'll even get a letter from Mr. Bootsie Tunabreath," said Boo.

"That's not my cat's name!" Laurel-Ann corrected. "His name is Mr. Cuddle Fluff."

Boo shook her head in disbelief. "And you actually admit that in public." She looked at me again. "Who's writing you so many letters, anyway? Do you have your own private fan club or something?"

"Not at all," I said. I couldn't wait to get out the door, but Laurel-Ann cornered me before I could escape.

"Hey, Kayla—do you want to go to tennis with me? We could play doubles together. If you don't know how to play, that's okay. The counselors will teach you some strokes to start out. I'm not very good, but I'm trying to get better. But what do I know—maybe you're a great tennis player and—"

"Um, no thanks. I actually went to tennis this morning. But maybe we can do something together another time." I slid past her to the door. Laurel-Ann looked really disappointed.

But I had gone this morning. I'd watched the Side A girls argue their way through a three-person match. It seemed like Devon and Maggie both wanted Chris's undivided attention. They hadn't even noticed I was there, which was just fine with me.

Outside on Middler Line, girls were pouring out of the doors of their cabins and talking and laughing. It was hard to believe it was only the second day of camp. Already everyone seemed to have friends.

But there were worse things than being alone. What if there'd been a giant mudslide that had trapped all of us inside the cabin together? Then I'd have to listen to Laurel-Ann talk while Boo gave me the third degree in the middle of a fight between Devon and Maggie over who was going to get Chris's attention. Wayward would tell us to "be Zen," and Gloria would want us all to get along.

So if I had to choose between spending the afternoon with all my cabinmates during a giant mudslide or being alone, there was really no competition.

I stopped in the bathrooms, which I could not get used to calling Solitary. As I pushed open the door to one stall, I glanced around quickly because yesterday I'd seen a spider crawling down the wall.

I'd just fastened the little hook into the eye to lock the door when I heard several girls walk in. I probably wouldn't have noticed except one word caught my attention.

"Who? Kayla? What makes you think that?"

Hearing my own name made my heart pound. I held my breath and listened.

"Shhh! Lots of things. Number one: her clothes. Everything she wears is . . ."

There were voices, several voices. I couldn't tell how many. Two, three, maybe even more than that. But they were whispering, so it was hard for me to recognize them.

". . . isn't it weird about all that mail and . . ."

". . . some special reason to make phone calls . . ."

"Yeah, and where is she really from? I mean, she obviously isn't . . ."

I was pressing my ear against the crack of the door, straining to hear.

Who was it? Boo? Shelby? Betsy? I just couldn't tell. And it didn't help that now their voices were drowned out by other sounds. Someone had turned on the water at one of the faucets. Then there was the sound of the paper towel roller being rotated.

I pictured all seven of the Cabin 4 girls standing around washing their hands. Talking, talking, talking. About me.

Footsteps. They had all walked out, and everything was quiet again.

Everything except for the sound of my pounding heartbeat.

CHAPTER 5

Wednesday, June 18

"Lay down your rifles and put your safeties on," Jamie, the riflery counselor, told us. We put our rifles down and slid the safeties forward. "Okay to retrieve your targets."

There were about nine of us at the riflery range, and we all climbed off the wooden platform and walked across the clearing to take down our targets. I was thrilled when I got to mine. In the center of the paper target was a black circle with a bunch of little rings inside it. I'd hit one bullet in the eight-point ring, which was just two rings away from the center bull's-eye. Not bad, considering this was the first time I'd ever shot a gun.

The riflery range was hidden in the woods down a little dirt path. There was a wooden platform with a roof over it and a row of mattresses for us to lie on. That had surprised me—that we were supposed to lie down on our stomachs and prop ourselves up on our elbows to fire the rifles.

Jamie had given us some basic instructions on how to load the rifles, aim, and fire, and then we'd spent the rest of the activity period on target practice. It was actually pretty cool.

Off in the distance we could hear the bell ringing to signal the end of activities. As I walked along the dirt path that led back into camp, I was in a good mood. It was sunny and warm, and I passed by a few girls in swimsuits wrapped up in towels who were just leaving the lake. One of them made eye contact with me as I passed by.

"Excuse me! Can I have your—"

"Stop! That's mean."

I glanced over my shoulder to see what was going on. The tall girl named JD was laughing and trying to say something, but she couldn't because her friend Courtney had covered JD's mouth with her hand.

JD pulled Courtney's hand away and shouted at me, "Can I have your autograph?"

Courtney looked embarrassed. "Just ignore her." She frowned at JD and shook her head.

I stared at them, trying to figure out what was going on.

"You'll have to excuse her. She's just being a goofball," another one of her friends said. JD seemed to think something was hysterically funny, but her friends were holding her back. Once they were a few steps ahead of me, they started talking again, but they still gave me looks as they walked away.

What was that all about? There was obviously some kind of inside joke they were all in on. And that joke had something to do with me.

I could feel my stomach tying itself in knots. Why? Why were they talking about me? It seemed like they were making fun of me.

But I barely knew those girls.

It was bad enough that the girls in my own cabin had been talking about me. I'd tried not to think about it because every time I did, I just got upset. I'd been staying away from them as much as possible and going to activities alone.

But now what? Was it starting to spread? Autograph? Why would she say that? Every muscle in my body was starting to tense up as I walked.

Was it my clothes? It seemed like everyone was always talking about how nice and new my clothes were.

I was getting sick of all the attention people around here paid to clothes. Yesterday Devon had made fun of Maggie for wearing the same shirt two days in a row. And during evening program last night, I'd listened to Jennifer and Reb, a couple of girls from Cabin 1, laughing at another girl, Melissa, behind her back because she was wearing a T-shirt with ponies on it.

It seemed like no one's clothes were right. I didn't realize how lucky I'd been at school, having to wear a uniform.

I just wanted to be alone and practice. I knew that would make me feel better. I ran up to the cabin and grabbed my sheet music out of my trunk. Then I went straight to the lodge.

The minute I sat down on the bench, I could feel myself relaxing a little. This piano was old and out of tune. The high B and C didn't work, but it was better than nothing.

I loved having the whole empty lodge to myself. A warm breeze blew in through the open windows, and as I started playing, the sound of the notes filled the high ceiling overhead.

I ran through a few scales and some left-hand arpeggios to warm up. It seemed strange to be practicing without my metronome. My teacher, Ms. Lerman, always wanted me to practice with it, but in the craziness of packing, I'd forgotten to bring it with me.

I loved Ms. Lerman. She was really challenging, but she was also cool. I was going to miss my piano teacher so much. I wondered what my new teacher would be like.

Thinking about Ms. Lerman reminded me of my first piano recital with her, when I'd played the first movement of Beethoven's Moonlight Sonata. So now I started playing that piece from memory.

I loved the way it started off pianissimo. "Soft and still as the night itself," Ms. Lerman would remind me. It wasn't very hard to play, but there were a couple of places where I had to stretch a ninth, and that was tough to do.

But I really liked this piece, and sometimes when I was playing, I almost felt like I was in a trance.

Until I heard the sound of a board creaking behind me. I glanced over my shoulder and saw Shelby leaning against the open door.

"Don't stop. I like that song," she told me. "Do you mind if I listen?"

"Of course not," I said, although I did kind of prefer being alone while I practiced.

Shelby moved quietly across the floor until she was standing by the edge of the piano.

I liked Shelby better than nosy Boo and chatty Laurel-Ann. But I wondered if she'd been one of the girls talking about me in the bathroom the other day. I thought I'd recognized her voice. I just couldn't be sure.

I started over at the beginning. I concentrated on keeping the triplet line flowing and was deep into the movement when I heard Shelby making little sniffling noises.

I glanced up. Was she actually crying? She was. She really was. I looked down at the keyboard and acted like I hadn't noticed.

Should I say something? Stop playing? Try to comfort her?

I didn't really know what to do. So I played to the end of the movement. Then I just sat there quietly with my fingers still resting lightly on the keyboard. Neither one of us said anything at first.

Shelby rubbed her eyes roughly with both hands. She'd stopped sniffling, and I could tell she was trying to get her tears under control. "My mom always played that song on our piano," she said finally.

"It's one of my favorite songs too," I said. I fingered the keys delicately so I wouldn't have to look at her. "You know, I feel homesick too. Especially at night."

There was a long pause. "I'm not homesick. I'll tell you something." Shelby pushed her bangs out of her eyes and gave me a quick look. "Can you keep a secret?"

"Of course," I said, feeling my heartbeat speed up. Was this something I really wanted to hear?

"My mom died last year. Cancer."

I sat there frozen, my fingers hovering just above the keys. I'd made a little sound when I'd sucked in my breath, but now I was absolutely silent. I had to swallow before I could say anything.

"I'm so sorry," I said in a scratchy voice that didn't sound like me at all.

It was just so awful. And here I'd been feeling sorry for myself because we were moving and I had to switch piano teachers.

"Please don't tell anyone, okay? I don't like to talk about it. And when people find out, they're like, 'Oh my God, that's so sad!' That just makes it worse."

"I promise I won't tell anyone." I fingered a few chords very softly so I'd at least have something to do with my hands.

Shelby slowly let out her breath. "I think I feel better

now. It was sad hearing that song again, but it reminded me of her. And that's good."

I cleared my throat. "I try to practice a little every day. I don't mind if you come in and listen."

She smiled at me. "Thanks. Maybe I will."

I was glad that she trusted me enough to tell me something so private.

There were already enough gossipy girls in this camp. And one thing I was absolutely sure about: I was never going to be one of them.

CHAPTER 6

Thursday, June 19

"Is this the group going to Angelhair Falls?" I asked. About five or six girls were standing around waiting in a shady spot behind the dining hall. I'd heard this was where we were supposed to meet for the hike to a nearby waterfall.

"Yep, you're in the right place," said Rachel Hoffstedder, one of the hiking counselors. She had short brown hair, and I was about two or three inches taller than she was, but she gave me a friendly smile. All the counselors seemed nice. Much nicer than the campers.

The girls in the group were talking and laughing together, but I stood a few feet away from them and kept quiet. I was glad nobody from our cabin was going on this hike.

Things hadn't gotten any better. It seemed like every time I walked into the cabin, everyone would stop talking. I was almost positive they were talking about me. But I still had no idea what they were saying. I tried not to think about it.

This was only temporary. One whole week was almost over. Meanwhile, I kept busy by going to activities.

"Okay, this looks like a pretty good group," Rachel said. "Everybody stick together and stay on the trail."

She led us up the hill past the camp office into a patch of woods, where a little dirt trail was visible among the trees. Pretty soon the bright afternoon sunlight was blocked out by all the tree branches overhead as the trail wound deeper and deeper into the forest.

Under our feet was a thick layer of dead leaves that made the ground feel spongy. The trail was so overgrown that twigs and branches were constantly scratching my arms and legs as I pushed past them. I learned to reach out for a branch in front of me and hold on to it as I passed so I didn't get swatted.

"Remember two years ago when we came on this

hike?" a girl named Darcy asked her friend Nicole. They were just behind me on the trail.

"Oh, yeah! Wasn't that the time you slipped in and got your shoes soaking wet as soon as we got to the falls?"

They kept talking, and even though I wasn't the least bit interested in their conversation, it was impossible for me not to overhear them. They seemed like best friends, and of course that made me think of Danielle.

What would it be like if Danielle or one of my other good friends like Maricela or Emily was here with me right now? For a second I imagined all these strange girls replaced with my own friends instead. A tight feeling came into my throat, and I suddenly wished I'd never come on this hike.

It would've been better to spend the afternoon alone in the lodge, playing the piano. Why was it that I never felt lonely when I was alone, only when I was with other people?

It could be worse, I reminded myself. We could get lost out here and have to depend on our own survival skills. And if you were ever lost in the woods, you'd have to eat disgusting things like caterpillars and grubs and tree bark. I knew that for a fact because I'd seen it on TV.

And since I could never eat those things, even if my life depended on it, I'd waste away to nothing. But being the skinniest in the group might be helpful in some cases. Like during a bear attack. But then it would be tough to explain why I was the only one who didn't get eaten.

So I was glad we weren't all starving right now and living off tree bark. And even though I didn't really like these strange girls who weren't my friends, they didn't deserve to be turned into a bear family's picnic lunch. So thinking about that helped me to enjoy this nice little hike through the woods, where I was absolutely positive that no one was going to get eaten. At least 99 percent positive. I concentrated on listening to the birds singing and tried not to think about that other 1 percent.

"How much farther to the falls?" a girl near the front of the line asked Rachel.

Rachel suggested that we all try to be the first one to hear the water, and whoever heard it first would get a prize.

"Oh, hi!" the girl behind me said suddenly. I'd stopped to hold a stray branch back so she wouldn't get hit with it. "You're Kayla, right?" She sped up a little so she could walk beside me on the path.

"Yes," I answered. It made me nervous that she

seemed so excited to be talking to me all of a sudden. Just a minute ago, she'd been chatting away with Nicole and Darcy.

"I've heard about you! It's really nice to meet you. I'm Brittany." She was Asian, with short black hair, and she was acting really friendly, like she already knew me.

"Heard about me?" I asked. "What have you heard?"

Something about the way I said that wiped the smile right off Brittany's face. "Oh, just . . . you're from California, right?" She glanced at me nervously. She seemed to realize she'd just said something that upset me.

"No," I said, shaking my head. "I'm not from California."

"Oh, I guess—maybe I've got you mixed up with someone else. I'm new this year, so I'm just starting to meet people."

Was that stupid states game from the first night coming back to haunt me again? At least she hadn't asked me if I was from Tennessee.

"Is this your first year too?" asked Brittany. "How do you like it so far?" I could tell she was trying to change the subject. She really did seem nice, and I felt bad for snapping at her. So we talked for a few minutes about our first impressions of Pine Haven. I acted like I was enjoying myself, because like I said, it could be worse.

The girls in front of us had slowed down a little, and we could hear Rachel at the front of the line calling out to the rest of us. "We're getting close to the falls now. Everyone keep your ears open. Whoever hears the sound of the falls first will get the prize. And it's going to be delicious!"

"Oh, cool. Let's listen for it," said Brittany excitedly. "I hope it's chocolate."

Then I noticed something. A girl named Erin who had been at the front of the line with Rachel had now moved toward the back. She was whispering something to Darcy and Nicole. When they noticed I was watching them, they smiled at me all innocently.

Now what? Were these girls talking about me too? Was everyone in camp talking about me, spreading more rumors? I swatted a branch out of my way and sped up a little to get away from all these gossipy girls.

"Getting closer. Keep listening for the sound of the waterfall," Rachel reminded us. So everyone got quiet and listened. That was the most wonderful sound I'd heard all day. The sound of girls not gabbing. It was amazing that these Pine Haven girls didn't go around with their tongues in slings. You'd think they'd sprain them all the time, considering they gave them constant workouts.

And then I heard it. Or I was pretty sure I did. The sound of the waterfall. No one else said anything, so at first I thought I was imagining it. But then I was sure of it.

"Wait. I think I can hear running water," I said to Rachel. I was surprised that I was actually the first to mention it. Couldn't they all hear it by now?

"Kayla gets the prize, since she was the first one to hear it," Rachel said, loud enough for everyone to hear.

Brittany came up to me and flashed a friendly smile. "I was just about to say something too! But that's cool you heard it first."

I wasn't feeling quite so mad now. "If it's candy, I'll give it to my little sister." Samantha would love that. Come to think of it, Samantha would love any kind of prize, so I'd give her whatever it was.

Rachel led us through the woods until the falls came into view. It wasn't the big, huge waterfall I'd been expecting, but it was still really beautiful. Rachel explained that it was called Angelhair Falls because of the way the rushing water poured across the rocks in little streams.

We were at the base of the falls where the water was churning into a pool of white foam. Now the sound of the rushing water was really loud, and we had to raise our voices as we talked. Standing at the edge of the creek, I could see how shallow the water was and how it rippled over all the smooth brown rocks lying in the bed of the creek. The air smelled damp and clean here next to the waterfall, and the temperature was several degrees cooler.

I turned around to face Rachel. "Okay. What's my prize?"

Rachel's eyes got wide when she looked at me. "We throw you in!" she yelled. And then the next thing I knew, she and three of the girls ran up and grabbed me. Erin and Rachel had me by the feet, Darcy and Nicole had me by the hands, and they were dragging me to the creek.

I couldn't help it. I screamed, because now they were swinging me back and forth! Were they really going to throw me in? "One . . . two . . . three!" Rachel yelled. I held my breath and braced myself for the cold splash.

But they just set me down. Right at the edge of the creek. I could hear everyone around me laughing, but I sat there paralyzed. My heart wouldn't stop pounding. Rachel winked at me. "You okay?"

I nodded. The only thing I could say was, "Now I'm wet," because even though they hadn't thrown me in, they'd put me down in some soft moss, and I could feel the dampness seeping through my shorts.

All the other girls had kicked off their shoes and socks and were wading into the rushing water of the stream. Rachel took off her backpack and pulled out a glass jar that had a bright orange salamander inside it. She told us about how she'd caught it yesterday to use in the skit for evening program last night, but now it was time to let it go.

I hadn't moved from my spot. Erin walked over and sat down beside me. "We'd never throw you in. That trick gets played on a new girl every year. Now you know. So next year, you'll have to come back on this hike, and then you can be in on the joke," she explained.

"That'll be fun," I said, since she was being so friendly. But I couldn't help thinking that for me, there wasn't going to be a next year.

CHAPTER 7

Being almost thrown in the creek was bad enough. Then on the hike back, we had to sing.

And we didn't just sing a regular song. No, Rachel thought it would be fun to do a round. So she made us sing a song I remembered from my days as a Brownie.

"Make new friends, but keep the old—one is silver and the other gold."

We had to keep singing that over and over with some of us starting it off, and then another bunch coming in midway through, and the last bunch coming in at the end.

"Make new friends, but keep the old—one is silver and the other gold. Make new friends, but keep the old—one is silver and the other gold. Make new friends, but keep the old—one is silver and the other gold."

The problem with singing a round was that it wasn't like a regular song that had an end to it. You kept singing it again and again, and nobody was ever sure when it was okay to stop.

And I really wasn't in the mood to listen to a song like that at the moment, much less sing it. My shorts were wet, I wasn't interested in making any new friends, and I didn't like being reminded to keep my old friends when I was about to move hundreds of miles away from them. Finally we all just sort of tapered off and stopped singing.

"Hey, everyone see this?" asked Rachel, pointing to a plant growing by the side of the path. "Three leaves. You know what that means."

"Poison ivy," said Erin.

"Yep, stay away from that stuff," Rachel warned.

Was that the next trick they were going to play? Grab the new girl and throw her into some poison ivy? But as we walked on past, no one rushed me, so I relaxed a little bit.

"Are you sure you're okay?" asked Brittany, catching up with me on the path.

"Yeah, I'm fine," I said. I felt like I had to put on a

semi-happy face so people didn't think I was upset about almost being thrown in. The last thing I wanted was for this group to go back to camp and start talking about me too. If they weren't already.

"Honestly, I was this close to being the one to say I could hear the waterfall. Then it would've been me instead of you." She glanced at me. "They didn't hurt you or anything, did they?"

"No, it just surprised me."

"Me too!" said Brittany. "I was so sure they were going to throw you in! I think Erin was planning it with Darcy and Nicole. They were being all secretive right before we got to the waterfall. Erin talked me into coming on this hike." She laughed. "I think she was hoping it was going to be me!"

"Really?" I asked. "I thought they were talking about me." I felt a little nervous admitting that to Brittany, but she seemed nice. And she'd obviously heard something about me before she met me. "I get the feeling that lots of people are talking about me," I added softly.

Brittany was quiet for a minute. We came to a spot in the trail where we had to climb over a fallen tree. "What makes you think that?" she asked, once we'd both scrambled over it.

Nicole and Darcy were behind us, but they weren't

talking very much now. Ahead of us were Erin and Isabel, the girl who'd failed the swim test on the first day. She seemed really shy, so it was probably good that she hadn't been the victim like me.

"Well, I heard some girls in my cabin talking about me the other day. I know it was me because I heard them say my name." I couldn't believe I'd just told Brittany that, but there was something about her that made me think I could trust her.

Brittany didn't say anything, but she had this look on her face like she knew exactly what I was talking about.

"Do you mind if I ask you what you've heard about me?" I said finally.

"Well . . . ," she started off. "I heard you were from Hollywood. Your mom's a movie star, and you answer all her fan mail."

If Brittany had broken a branch off a nearby tree and clubbed me over the head with it, I couldn't have been more stunned.

"What?" I yelled. "Who told you that?"

"Oh, and you're also trying to keep your identity a secret because you're pretending to be from Tennessee or something?" Her voice rose up like a question.

"That's crazy! My mom works at a TV station, but she's not a movie star. At all. I've never even been to

Hollywood, but some friends of mine just took a trip there and sent me some postcards."

It made me mad to hear what kinds of crazy rumors were going around, but in some ways it was a relief to finally know what people were saying about me.

Brittany let out a little embarrassed laugh. "I know. It sounds unbelievable now that I'm telling you about it." She ducked under a low-hanging tree branch. "Watch out for that," she warned.

"Who told you all this stuff?" I asked. "None of it's true, by the way."

"I heard some girls talking about it before evening program the other night," said Brittany.

"Which girls?" I asked. "What did they look like?"

"Hmm. I'm not really sure. I don't know too many names yet."

"Was one of them chubby? With blond hair and glasses?"

"I don't think so," she answered, but her voice didn't sound all that convincing.

"Well, just don't believe everything you hear, all right?" I warned her.

Brittany laughed. "I won't. Trust me!" She gave me a quick look. "You're not mad, are you?"

"No, I'm actually glad I found out. Thanks for telling me."

I tried to remind myself that it could've been a much worse rumor, something really embarrassing. Like the rumor that was going around my school last year that William Takashi and Kelsey Vandamere had been kissing under the bleachers during a basketball game and their braces had locked together.

The story was that they'd tried to scream, but no one could hear them over the noise of the game, and then everyone had gone home and they'd gotten locked inside the gym and a janitor had found them later. He'd called the fire department and it took two hours to get them separated. They both denied it, but they both did have braces, and they did like each other. I was never sure what to believe.

When we got back into camp, Erin came over to talk to me. "Hey, thanks for being a good sport. Sorry we got your shorts dirty." She glanced at my backside. "They look new. Next time, you should probably wear old clothes on a hike," she suggested.

"Good idea," I said. That was it. The first chance I got, I'd buy some Pine Haven T-shirts at the camp store. Maybe then people would stop talking about how I dressed.

Erin and Brittany invited me to go swimming during afternoon free time, but I wanted to visit Samantha and get my practice in, so I told them some other time.

The cabin was almost empty when I walked in, but not empty enough. Betsy was on Side A, and Laurel-Ann was lying on her cot, writing a letter.

"Oh my gosh, what happened?" she gasped when she saw how dirty my shorts were.

"Nothing," I said. "I just got back from a hike."

All I wanted to do was change clothes and get out of there as fast as possible before Laurel-Ann sucked me into a conversation.

It reminded me of the corn maze at the Illinois State Fair, with all these twists and turns and dead ends. Once you got stuck in the maze, it was almost impossible to find your way out again. A conversation with Laurel-Ann was like that: Once she pulled you in, it was hard to get out.

She'd been trying really hard to be my friend, maybe because she felt sorry for me for being new. What she didn't seem to get was that I was perfectly happy going to activities by myself.

"Was it the Angelhair Falls hike?" she asked. "Were you the one they pretended to throw in? Gosh, I wish I'd known you were going on that hike. I would've told you that they do that every year to a new girl. And what if those stains don't come out of your shorts?"

"It's no big deal," I said. "It's just . . ." I sat down on my bed. "Don't tell Boo, all right? Once she hears this story, she'll probably tell everyone something completely different."

I could just imagine Boo's version of what had happened to me on the hike. Something about how I'd gone on a mad rampage when someone made a comment about my clothes. The whole group had to tie me up and toss me into the water to cool me down. Then I'd gotten so mad I started a forest fire to send smoke signals to my movie star parents to come rescue me in their private jet plane.

Laurel-Ann sat up and looked at me. "What do you mean?"

"I think Boo's been talking about me behind my back," I said. There was a good chance that Laurel-Ann already knew this, because she might've been one of the girls in the bathroom that day. But I didn't care at this point. I wanted all this gossiping to stop.

Laurel-Ann covered her mouth with one hand. "Really? That's terrible! What's she been saying?"

"She's going around telling people my mother is a movie star and I'm trying to hide my identity. And I live in Hollywood."

"It's so rude the way she asks you all those questions.

And she's always making fun of people. She doesn't like me. I know she doesn't. Has she been saying anything about me?" She plucked nervously at the rubber bands on her braces.

"No, I try to avoid her as much as possible."

"You don't really live in Hollywood, do you?" asked Laurel-Ann.

"Of course not! Some of my friends are on a school trip there right now, that's all. They sent me postcards. My mother works at a TV station. She's not a movie star."

We heard the screen door open, and my least favorite cabinmate walked in. "What's going on?" Boo asked us.

"Nothing," Laurel-Ann said.

Boo stared at us. "Why are y'all giving me such dirty looks? I didn't sneeze in your Cap'n Crunch."

"We're not giving you dirty looks," said Laurel-Ann, grinning at Boo with a fake smile. "We're just talking. Not about anything. Just totally boring stuff." Then she looked worried. "I didn't mean you're boring, Kayla. I meant Boo would be bored."

"You got that right. I'm bored already." Boo sat down on her bed and pulled off her tennis shoes and socks. "I just came from Solitary. And guess who's locked in a stall crying her eyes out again?"

"Who?" asked Laurel-Ann with wide eyes.

"You're no fun. You're supposed to guess," said Boo, tossing one of her dirty socks up on Shelby's bed.

"Is it Shelby? Really? She's so homesick," said Laurel-Ann. "I think that's so sad. We should try to cheer her up when she comes back. She just needs to make some friends, and then she'll—"

"She just needs to grow up." Boo said, tossing her other dirty sock on Shelby's bed. "I can't believe that someone our age acts like that. I started coming to camp when I was eight, and I never got homesick. She's twelve. Get over it already."

I stood up and brushed the dirty socks off Shelby's bed. They fell to the floor. "Did it ever occur to you that maybe she's not homesick?" I snapped. It made me furious to hear Boo making fun of Shelby and spreading even more gossip.

"It's obvious she's homesick! She cries herself to sleep every night." Boo stood up and tossed her shoes on the bottom shelf by the door.

I'm ordinarily not a violent person, but at that moment I wanted to grab one of those shoes and shove it down Boo Bauer's throat. "Maybe she has a good reason for crying! Maybe it has absolutely nothing to do with being homesick!"

Boo stood frozen in place, staring at me. "You know something, don't you?"

"I don't know anything." I turned away from her. My dirty shorts were lying on the top of my trunk, so I stuffed them in my laundry bag.

"Ha! Oh yes, you do! I can tell by the way you're acting."

I crossed my arms over my chest. I hated the way Boo was making me feel right now, like she could see right through me. And I did feel like I was hiding some deep, dark secret.

"It could be something horrible!" said Laurel-Ann. "Like maybe her dog died. Or maybe it got hit by a car and it's suffering, and her parents wrote her and told her that they need to put the dog down, but she's begging them to wait till she gets home so she can say good-bye, but all the time she realizes—"

"Hyphen, where do you come up with all this stuff?"

"I've got an idea! Maybe I should ask her if she has a dog and see what her reaction is. If she bursts into tears, then we'll know the truth." Laurel-Ann twisted one braid around her finger with a hopeful look on her face.

Boo gazed at me, and now all of a sudden she was really serious. "Is it something about her mom? Yesterday I overheard her talking to Gloria. She was saying something about how she missed her mom."

"It's none of our business!" I blurted out. "This is something private that Shelby doesn't want to talk about." I couldn't believe that Boo was standing there, admitting to us that she was in the habit of eavesdropping on other people's conversations.

"Oh my gosh! That's it, isn't it?" Boo walked over and sat down on her cot, looking stunned. "I thought she was just homesick. I didn't realize something had happened to her mom."

Laurel-Ann was staring at me too. "I guess her dog's okay then."

"You've got butterscotch pudding where your brain's supposed to be!" Boo snapped at Laurel-Ann. "Can't you see this is serious?" Boo turned back to me. "Kayla, you obviously know what it is. Her mom's not dead or anything really bad like that, is she?"

I clamped my jaw shut and refused to say anything. I'd promised Shelby, and I wasn't about to break that promise, especially not to satisfy Boo Bauer's curiosity.

"Oh, wow! Oh, wow! That's it, isn't it? I can tell by the look on your face!"

"You better not say anything to Shelby!" I hissed. "If you spread rumors about her, I'll . . ." I couldn't think of what to threaten her with.

So I went to my trunk and grabbed my sheet music. I had to get out of there, fast.

"Kayla, wait!" Boo called to me. "Just tell me if it's true!"

But I headed straight for the door without answering.

I'd promised Shelby! I'd sworn I'd never tell anyone! And I hadn't . . . exactly. I felt like Boo had dragged it out of me.

But maybe she'd keep her mouth shut for once. Maybe she wouldn't go around talking about Shelby to everyone the way she'd talked about me.

Maybe.

But then again, maybe not.

CHAPTER 8

Saturday, June 21

"I told you not to tell!" Shelby yelled at me.

I'd been sitting at the piano, enjoying a few minutes alone, when she'd come storming through the door and confronted me.

I looked up at her. "I didn't tell! I swear I didn't." My fingers hovered over the keyboard, but I'd stopped in the middle of the piece I'd been practicing.

"Then how come everybody knows now? It seems like the whole camp has found out!" Shelby propped her thin arms on the top of the piano and glared at me.

I'd have to tell her what really happened and just hope she wouldn't still be mad at me. "I didn't tell anyone, but the other day, Boo sort of . . . guessed."

"Guessed? How could she guess?" Shelby brushed her bangs out of her eyes. Her hair was wet, like she'd just come from the shower.

"Well, she was laughing at you for crying at night. All I said was that you might have a good reason for crying. And then she started grilling me. I never told her! I promise. You can ask Laurel-Ann if you don't believe me. She was there."

"You swore you'd keep it a secret!" Shelby's face twisted into a frown. She refused to even look at me.

"Boo's the one who's been going around telling everyone. Not me. Do you know she actually admitted to Laurel-Ann and me that she was eavesdropping on you and Gloria one day? She said she'd, quote, 'overheard' the two of you talking in the cabin."

Shelby stared at me in disbelief. "She actually said that?"

"Yes! I'm telling you, she's a terrible gossip. She's been talking about lots of people, not just you. So don't take it too personally."

Shelby shook her head. "She does tease me all the time. Like, when I walk by her, she'll make these sniffling sounds, and when I look at her, she just says, 'Sorry. Allergies.' Like it's some big joke or something that she's heard me crying."

"You have nothing to be ashamed of, Shelby. Don't pay any attention to what Boo or anyone else says. You shouldn't be embarrassed."

Shelby let out a slow breath. "Thanks."

"How'd you find out? Did you start hearing crazy rumors about yourself?" I wondered how Boo had taken Shelby's story and twisted it around till there wasn't any truth left at all.

She looked at me with raised eyebrows. "No. Not crazy rumors. Just people all of a sudden wanted to talk about their dead grandparents and cats and dogs every time I was around. I sort of figured out what was going on that way."

I stared down at the keyboard. "I'm really sorry. That Boo Bauer! Why can't she learn to keep her mouth shut?"

Shelby gave me a sly look. "Maybe we should start spreading rumors about her. Give her a taste of her own medicine."

I smiled slightly. I was glad that Shelby didn't seem mad at me anymore, but I didn't really want to get caught up in something like that.

"I don't know. I don't like all this gossiping. Once a rumor starts, it gets spread around so fast. It's like the plague. It's a good thing it's just words and not deadly bacteria. The whole camp would be wiped out in one afternoon."

Shelby laughed and snapped her fingers. "That's it! Bubonic Boo! Maybe that's where that nickname comes from! I mean, what is her real name, anyway?"

"I have no idea. I've never heard anyone call her anything else."

Shelby was chuckling evilly. "Bubonic Boo. I love it! I'm going to start calling her that."

"Hey, what's it like on Middler Line now?" I asked, trying to change the subject. "I came down here to get away from all the craziness."

"It's gotten worse," Shelby said. "Nobody's at activities. Everyone's in line for the showers. I was lucky to get one when I did. People are running around trying to borrow clothes. It's insane."

"Tell me about it. I've had girls I barely know ask to borrow my clothes," I told her. Not that I minded. For once, people weren't giving me a hard time about my new clothes, so I was happy to let them borrow whatever they wanted.

Ordinarily, late afternoons at camp were fairly peaceful. After activities were over for the day, we had free time to do whatever we wanted before dinner.

But this afternoon was different. Supposedly, tonight

we were having our first dance with the boys of Camp Crockett, and suddenly Middler Line had turned into a madhouse.

I'd been practicing Mozart's Piano Sonata no. 16 in C Major, so I started playing it again. Shelby came and sat down on the bench next to me while I played. It wasn't long, though, before other girls started coming to the lodge with their hair dryers to look for electric outlets. Since the cabins didn't have any plugs, the lodge was just about the only place in camp where people could use anything electric.

Shelby's friend Claudia appeared first. They were in a swimming class together that was supposed to train them to be lifeguards.

Then Chris and Devon came in to use Devon's hair straightener, and a few minutes later Brittany, the girl I'd met on the hike the other day, showed up.

It was getting noisy in here with the sounds of the hair dryers, but I'd promised myself I'd try to squeeze in an hour a day. I kept working on Mozart. He had thought of this piece as being for beginners, and in some ways it was, with lots of rippling scales up and down played at an allegro tempo. But Ms. Lerman had warned me not to be fooled by the fact that it was called Sonata facile, which meant easy.

"Wow, you're good," said Chris, running a brush through her dark, wavy hair.

"Thanks. It's horribly out of tune, though," I told her.

"Oh, Kayla, did you hear about the hiking trip next week?" Brittany asked me. "It's an overnight. Doesn't that sound cool? We take backpacks and sleeping bags and spend the night outside. Rachel's my counselor. She was telling Erin and me about it."

"Really?" I asked. "That sounds fun." My family had never camped out before. Since we'd always lived in cities, we weren't really outdoorsy types. Whenever I saw people camping out on TV, I always wanted to try it.

"Yeah, Erin and I are definitely going. You should too. We'll cook out over a campfire and tell ghost stories and everything!"

"I'll think about it. Thanks for telling me," I told Brittany. Chris and Devon went back to the cabin to get dressed. Shelby asked me to wait for her while she dried her hair.

"Are you sure you're not mad?" I asked Shelby as we walked back to the cabin together. "I'm really sorry about what happened."

Shelby shook her head. "No, I don't blame you. It's Boo. I'm going to get her back. Bubonic Boo. Want to help me?"

I shrugged. "I don't know. I'd be happy if she'd learn to keep her mouth shut."

We changed clothes for the dance, and then it was time for dinner. On the way to the dining hall, I was able to pull Samantha away from her friends for five minutes so I could say hi to her.

"Did you have a good day today?" I asked.

"Yes, but we don't get to go to the dance tonight. It's only for the Middlers and Seniors. Not the Juniors." She frowned at me with her arms crossed.

"Yeah, how is that fair?" said little redheaded Gracie, standing beside her.

"Sorry, I don't make the rules," I told them. I did feel bad for Samantha and her friend. But who cared about the dance?

All day I'd been happy thinking about one thing. One whole week was already over. Only three more to go.

CHAPTER 9

You'd think these girls had not seen boys for a year instead of a week. People were dressed up, wearing makeup and jewelry, and they were all so excited. The older girls, the Seniors, were staying at Pine Haven, and the boys their age were coming to them. But the Middlers were shuttled over to Camp Crockett to have our dance inside their dining hall.

When we first got there, the boys barely even noticed that we'd arrived. But already the music was playing, and all the girls were waiting around, whispering and talking together.

Shelby and I were standing together when Laurel-Ann walked up. Tonight she didn't have her hair in braids. Instead she was wearing it down, with a headband that matched the yellow Abercrombie shirt I'd loaned her.

"Is it okay if I hang out with y'all tonight?" she asked us. "It's sort of embarrassing to wait for a boy to ask you to dance. You're all by yourself, and the boys are probably thinking, 'What's wrong with her, anyway? Doesn't she have any friends? I don't want to dance with some loser.'"

"We don't have to wait for boys to ask us to dance. We can dance anytime we feel like it," Shelby told her. "The point is to have fun." She looked at me. "Kayla, I can tell you like to dance. Let's go. Why stand here waiting?"

"How can you tell I like to dance?" I asked.

Shelby laughed. "Because you're bouncing to the beat. Come on! Laurel-Ann, you too. I dare you!"

Shelby moved out among the dancers. "I love this song! How can anyone stand still when they hear it?"

I was so relieved that Shelby hadn't stayed mad at me. And it was nice to see her having a good time. She needed to have fun whenever she could. So I smiled at Laurel-Ann. "Let's go. It is a dance, you know." I weaved through the people who were just standing around, being boring.

"Woo-hoo!" Shelby shouted at me. "Can you play music like this on the piano?"

"Yes!" I said with a laugh. "This is easier to play than Mozart!"

There were lots of boys still lined up on one side of the dining hall, and across from them on the opposite side, all the Pine Haven girls were huddled together. About thirty or forty people were dancing in the middle. The counselors were just watching us all and laughing. They seemed to find us really entertaining.

Laurel-Ann was swaying a little back and forth to the music, but she kept looking all around the big dining hall. "Are you sure we don't look stupid?" she asked.

That made Shelby laugh, because Laurel-Ann did look kind of silly. "You're supposed to dance like you don't care how you look," she told her. "Wow, look at Lauren. Do you see her? The girl with the really blond hair? She's in my swimming class, and she's such a good dancer. I wish I could dance that well."

"You're a good dancer too," I said. For once, it was kind of fun to have friends to hang out with.

"I think people are laughing at us," said Laurel-Ann. She kept looking over her shoulder every five minutes.

"Laurel-Ann, believe me! Nobody's laughing at us," Shelby insisted.

"Are you thirsty? I'll get us some punch. Don't move

too far away or I won't be able to find you again," said Laurel-Ann, walking off through the crowd.

Shelby laughed. "She's such a goof! Have you ever heard anybody talk as much as she does?"

I shook my head. "I know! But she's still pretty nice."

A few minutes later, Laurel-Ann appeared, holding a paper cup in each hand. "Here, I got you some drinks. But you have to come with me. I've got to talk to you about something really, really important."

So Shelby and I followed her through the crowd to the edge of the dance floor. Shelby gulped down her drink while I took a couple of sips. It was the fruit punch drink they called "bug juice." Camp definitely had its own vocabulary for everything.

"What's wrong?" I asked.

Laurel-Ann shook her head. "This isn't a good place to talk. Let's go out on the porch."

She kept glancing around as if she was some kind of spy on a mission. So we all went out on the porch so she could tell us what was going on.

The porch was pretty crowded with people too. Lots of counselors from both camps were hanging out here and talking. But at least there wasn't music playing, so it was a little easier to hear each other.

"Okay, this is better," said Laurel-Ann, talking in a

low voice. "You'll never guess what happened when I went to get the drinks."

"You bumped into a boy, and when your eyes met, he said, 'Where have you been all my life?'" Shelby guessed. She was fidgeting, and I could tell she just wanted to get back inside.

"I wish! That didn't happen. I was at the table where all the refreshments are, and this girl came up to me and said, 'You and your friends think you look so cool, but you don't. It's so embarrassing that no boys will dance with you.'" Laurel-Ann paused and waited for this news to sink in. "Can you believe she said that?"

Shelby made a face. "Who cares? Who cares what other people say?" she said, but I could tell by the way she was frowning that it sort of bothered her.

It bothered me, too. Was that all girls did around here—talk about each other? I was getting really sick of this. I pictured every girl in camp with a big piece of duct tape across her mouth to solve this problem.

"Which girl? Point her out to us." I wondered if it was one of the girls at the lake that day, asking for my autograph.

Laurel-Ann sucked in her breath. "Why? What are you going to do to her?"

"We'll shove this paper cup in her mouth like this,"

said Shelby. She opened her mouth wide and sucked on the rim of her empty cup. Then she looked back and forth at Laurel-Ann and me. The paper cup was sticking out of her mouth like a giant white plug.

I couldn't keep from laughing over that, but Laurel-Ann looked worried. "You're not really going to do that, are you?"

"Well, probably not," I told her. "I can't believe how bad these Pine Haven girls are with talking about each other behind their backs."

Shelby pulled the cup out of her mouth. "I know! I'm surprised it wasn't Bubonic Boo who was talking about us, right, Kayla?"

"Bubonic Boo?" asked Laurel-Ann. "What's that supposed to mean?"

"That's Boo's new nickname, because she's spreading rumors around as fast as the plague," Shelby explained. "Lots of people have been her victims lately. But it's okay. We're plotting some way to get back at her."

Laurel-Ann gasped out loud. "Really? What are you going to do to her?"

Shelby chewed on the rim of her cup and looked thoughtful. "We don't know yet. But we're going to do something to her. You want in on it?"

Laurel-Ann's eyes grew three sizes, and she nodded

her head furiously. "Yes. Boo can't stand me. She's always saying mean things to me."

"Let's talk about this later," I suggested. "There are too many people around. I think we should go back inside."

"Okay," agreed Shelby. "And if we look silly dancing by ourselves, I'll just ask a boy to dance." She gave me a quick look. "I'll do it if you do."

"Maybe," I said.

"I don't think I'm going to dance for a while," said Laurel-Ann. "You two can go without me."

"Oh, come on," Shelby said. "Don't let other people stop you from having fun."

Just then a girl walked up to the three of us. "Hey, Rainbow Trout! I hear the fish are biting!" Laurel-Ann's face turned flaming red, and the girl let out an annoying laugh when she saw that. "What's the matter, Rainbow Trout? Did I embarrass you?"

She had long, stringy hair that she obviously hadn't even bothered to brush. It was tucked behind her ears, which made them look bigger than they probably were. And she was dressed in old, faded jeans and a baggy T-shirt. I'd seen her around camp all week, but I didn't know her name.

Laurel-Ann didn't answer her. "Let's get out of here,

okay?" she said to Shelby and me, and her voice sounded almost panicked. We followed her through the crowd of dancers.

"See ya later, Rainbow Trout!" the girl yelled after us.

"Who was that?" Shelby asked when we were far enough away.

Laurel-Ann's face was now just a bright shade of pink, but she still looked upset. "She's not somebody you want to know. Her name's Katherine Sperling. She was in my cabin last year." Laurel-Ann glanced nervously over her shoulder, as if she were afraid that Katherine was about to sneak up behind her.

"Is she the one who was talking about us?" asked Shelby. Her eyes scanned the crowd, keeping a lookout for Katherine.

Laurel-Ann stared at her for a second. At first I thought she wasn't going to answer, but then she said, "Yes! She's the one! What are you going to do to her?"

"We won't do anything to her," I told Laurel-Ann. "We just wanted to know who was making fun of us."

"Hey, what did she mean—Rainbow Trout? What was that all about?" Shelby asked.

Laurel-Ann shook her head. "Nothing." Then she clamped her mouth shut.

Shelby and I exchanged surprised looks. It wasn't

easy to shut Laurel-Ann's mouth, but that question had really done it.

"Oh, come on!" said Shelby with a laugh. "Why are you acting like that? There must be some kind of interesting story. You have to tell us."

"Never mind. It's nothing!" Laurel-Ann insisted. She refused to even look at us.

"You can tell us," Shelby assured her. "We promise we won't tell anyone else, right, Kayla?"

I shrugged. "If Laurel-Ann doesn't want to talk about it, we shouldn't force her."

Laurel-Ann let out a sigh. "Good! Because I don't want to talk about it!"

I had to admit, I was dying of curiosity. Rainbow Trout? That had to mean something. And even though I'd like to think that Shelby and I could keep Laurel-Ann's secret if she told us, I wasn't so sure. Secrets did have a way of slipping out.

And once they were out, you could never seem to get them back again.

CHAPTER 10

Monday, June 23

When Laurel-Ann and I met up with the group of hikers going on the overnight, Brittany ran up to me as soon as she saw me. "Oh, good! You decided to come. It's going to be great, don't you think?"

I smiled at her. "Definitely! I've been looking forward to this all weekend."

I was sort of disappointed that Shelby wasn't coming along, but she didn't want to miss her swimming class. Laurel-Ann had stuck close to me all weekend, so I'd given in and decided to let her be my friend. I did feel a little guilty, though, because if I had to choose, I'd probably pick Shelby over Laurel-Ann.

I wasn't thrilled about leaving poor Shelby all alone

with Boo, either. Shelby had decided to put an anonymous note in Boo's mailbox today addressed to "Bubonic Boo": *You better watch what you're spreading around. You could cause another plague.* I wasn't so sure I liked that idea, but I hadn't been able to talk her out of it. I just hoped that a war didn't break out between the two of them while Laurel-Ann and I were away on the overnight.

We'd already packed our backpacks with clothes and the other things we were going to need for the trip. Brittany's friend Erin was here too, and so were a couple of girls from Cabin 3—Natasha and Ashlin.

Natasha was a very petite girl with glasses, and like me, she was African American. She was always with her friend Ashlin, who had short, dark hair and a tomboy look about her.

"I hope everyone's ready for some serious hiking," Rachel said to us. She and Jerry, the hiking guide, were busy packing a first aid kit, some tarps, ropes, and other supplies into their backpacks.

One of the older girls, a Counselor Assistant in Training, or CAT, came out of the kitchen door carrying a big cardboard box full of sack lunches. Her name was Lori Espinoza, and she was going along on the overnight with us.

"Okay, everyone grab a lunch," Lori told us.

Laurel-Ann and I were putting our lunches away in our backpacks when I heard her gasp. "Oh, no! She can't be coming too!"

I looked around to see Katherine Sperling walking up with a backpack on her shoulders.

"I can't believe it!" Laurel-Ann whispered to me. "Katherine's going on this trip!" She glanced sideways at Katherine, who was now talking to Jerry. "Are you sure you still want to go?"

"Yes," I whispered back. "Don't worry about it. Just try to stay away from her." I slung my backpack over my shoulders and adjusted the straps.

"But this is an overnight! It's not like a regular hike that we'll be back from in a few hours." Laurel-Ann stood there, holding her backpack in front of her. "I'm seriously considering leaving. She hates me! She really does!"

"Look, she's not even paying any attention to you right now. It'll be fine," I tried to assure her.

"Okay, everybody ready? Let's go!" Rachel called out to the group. We followed her up the hill past Middler Lodge, where a trail led off into the woods. Since the trail was narrow and we were all wearing backpacks, we got into single file.

Rachel and Jerry were leading the way, followed by Ashlin, Natasha, and Katherine. Lori was behind her, and Brittany and Erin were in the middle. Laurel-Ann and I were in back because she'd waited to make sure Katherine was in front of us. So far, Katherine hadn't even so much as looked at Laurel-Ann, but that didn't seem to matter. She was still upset that Katherine was going along.

"Last year Katherine hated going to activities," Laurel-Ann said in a low voice from behind me. "She was always cabin-sitting, and she'd try to get me to stay with her, even though she knows it's against the rules to skip activities. But I know why she goes on hikes. She's got a huge crush on Jerry."

Jerry was a real outdoorsman. I could see how Katherine might have a crush on him, if she liked the rugged type.

"She has no friends," Laurel-Ann went on. "She really doesn't. I swear. I remember one time last year . . ." Laurel-Ann kept talking, and I just admired the beautiful scenery.

Everything was so green, and even though it was a sunny day, it was shady because of all the towering trees around us. Hiking along this trail with a backpack on my shoulders made me feel like a real explorer. I loved getting away from civilization and being close to nature like this.

It was a long hike, but I didn't mind at all. There was always something interesting to discover. We were hiking beside a little stream, and all the rocks around it were fuzzy and green with moss. When I reached down to touch it, I couldn't believe how thick and soft it felt.

After we'd been hiking for quite a while, Rachel called out from the front of the line, "Anyone ready for lunch?"

"Yes!" we shouted back.

Eating sack lunches outside was like being on a picnic, but the thing I liked best was that we all put our soft drinks into the stream we'd stopped beside so that the icy cold water would cool them down. It was Jerry's idea, and it worked really well, except Laurel-Ann's almost floated away because she forgot to put rocks around her can to keep it in place. While we waited for our drinks to get cold, we munched on peanut butter and honey sandwiches, chips, apples, and oatmeal raisin cookies.

"Everybody give me your trash," said Lori, going around with a trash bag to collect all the plastic bags, paper sacks, and apple cores. "Remember the rule— pack it in, pack it out."

Once we started hiking again, Laurel-Ann was upset that Katherine was now right in front of us. "Wonder if we're going to do any fishing after we set up camp?" Katherine said in a loud voice. She looked over her shoulder and flashed an evil grin at Laurel-Ann.

"Well, we don't have any fishing gear with us, so I doubt it," I heard Erin answer her. She and Brittany were ahead of us in the line.

"Oh, too bad. I hear our campsite is near a great fishing spot. Lots of rainbow trout. And we all know how much Laurel-Ann back there likes rainbow trout!" Then Katherine let out the most annoying laugh I'd ever heard.

"She's so mean!" Laurel-Ann whispered. "I never should've come on this trip."

"Just ignore her," I said softly. "If she sees how much it upsets you, she'll keep doing it."

What was this inside joke about rainbow trout? I was dying to find out. There had to be some way I could get Laurel-Ann to tell me the whole story.

Did Bubonic Boo know about it too? Probably. She seemed to know everything about everyone else's business.

The rest of the afternoon was pretty uneventful. Laurel-Ann was upset, and even though I did feel bad for her, it just so happened that when something was bothering her, she got really quiet. So I was actually able to enjoy the sound of the wind rustling through the leaves of the trees.

Late in the afternoon, we stopped at a clearing in the woods to set up camp. It was such a relief to finally take my backpack off. My new Pine Haven T-shirt was all sweaty from where my backpack had been, and I didn't realize how sore my shoulders and back were starting to feel.

We were in a beautiful spot. It was wooded all around us, but we'd come to a little clearing where the ground was flat and open. Down a sloping hill was the stream we'd been following for most of the hike. From our campsite, we could hear the sound of the water rippling over the rocks.

"Okay, ladies. We've got tarps to put under you to keep your sleeping bags dry," said Jerry. "Doesn't look like rain, so we'll be fine sleeping out in the open tonight." He looked up at the clear sky, visible through the trees above us.

So then we all got busy spreading out the tarps and laying out sleeping bags.

"We'll leave a spot in the middle for the campfire," Rachel told us.

"Good idea, Hoffstedder," Jerry agreed. "We need

some girls to gather firewood and some to find rocks to ring the fire with. And we need pine needles and twigs for kindling."

"I'll help you gather firewood, Jerry," said Katherine.

Laurel-Ann gave me a nudge. "See? What did I tell you?" She rolled her eyes at the way Katherine followed Jerry around.

Before long, we had our campsite set up. One thing I wasn't thrilled about was that we had to dig a latrine out in the woods behind a tree. But that was the only thing about camping I didn't like.

When it was time to make dinner, we lit the camp-fire, and Lori, Rachel, and Jerry showed us how to make campfire stew. We got busy cutting up carrots, onions, meat, and potatoes, and all the ingredients went into a collapsible metal pot that we then set into the hot coals so it could simmer.

It seemed like it took forever for the stew to cook, so we all took off our sweaty shoes and socks and played in the stream while we waited. The smell of the sim-mering stew made my stomach grumble. But when it was finally ready, it was hot and delicious.

"Did everyone leave room for dessert?" asked Rachel, pulling a bag of marshmallows out of her backpack.

"Yum!" said Ashlin. "Did you bring chocolate and graham crackers too?"

"You bet," answered Jerry. "You can't have a campfire without s'mores."

We scattered into the woods to find sticks to roast our marshmallows on. Lightning bugs were starting to come out of the grass, and their little lights flashed on and off like blinking signals all around us.

Lori had added more wood to the fire, so now it was a roaring blaze. We all stood around it with our sticks and held our marshmallows out to roast them. The fire was so hot it actually made me sweat, but I felt cool air on the backs of my bare legs. I was glad I'd put on a sweatshirt, because it was a chilly night. The smoke from the fire made my eyes water, but I loved the smell of the burning wood.

All of a sudden, Laurel-Ann's marshmallow burst into flames. "Oh, no! Oh, no!" she shrieked at the top of her lungs.

Katherine laughed so hard I thought she might lose her balance and fall into the fire. Laurel-Ann screamed and tossed the whole stick into the fire, and that made all of us laugh. I felt bad for her, but it really was a funny sight.

"That's okay," Jerry told her. "You can have this one." He

handed Laurel-Ann his stick. The marshmallow on the end of it was toasted to perfection. I could see Katherine frowning in the orange light of the fire. Those two really did seem to be mortal enemies for some reason.

"I've got a story," said Lori. "This is true, by the way." And then she told us about a cabin less than a mile from our campsite where a man's beautiful redheaded wife had gone out to pick berries one day and never returned. He'd searched for her for years, and sometimes he'd hear her voice calling to him, and sometimes he'd find a strand of red hair by the berry patch. But he never found her.

"But if you listen tonight, you might hear her calling, and when you wake up tomorrow, don't be surprised if you see a strand of red hair hanging from the trees."

Then Jerry told a ghost story that started off really scary but turned into a joke. After about three or four other ghost stories, Rachel said it was time to get some sleep.

Laurel-Ann had insisted that we put our sleeping bags as far away from Katherine as possible. Ashlin and Natasha had moved theirs close to ours, and luckily Katherine was on the other side of the campfire with Erin and Brittany.

After we crawled into our sleeping bags and turned

off our flashlights, I realized how completely pitch-dark it really was out here. By now the fire was just a bunch of red, glowing coals, and we could hear the sounds of the embers crumbling and popping as they slowly burned down.

All of a sudden, we heard a lot of loud laughter. We sat up and looked across the campsite to where Brittany, Erin, and Katherine were in their sleeping bags. They still had a flashlight on, and all three of them were laughing about something.

"I wonder what's so funny?" Natasha asked.

"I don't know," said Ashlin. "Something's sure cracking them up over there."

"I bet it's Katherine," Laurel-Ann whispered to us. "She's probably telling Brittany and Erin a bunch of lies about us."

"Well, if she is, they're funny lies," said Ashlin.

Another shriek of laughter made all of us sit up and try to see across the dark stretch of ground between our group and theirs. The beam of a flashlight was dancing all around, but we couldn't see anything else.

"Hey, keep it down over there," Rachel's voice called out.

"Okay. Sorry," we heard someone answer. Then things got quiet, and we all settled back down in our sleeping bags. The frogs were making that *burap, burap* sound, which I was actually sort of used to by now.

"Let me see it!" a voice said suddenly. And then there was a playful scream, followed by lots of laughing.

Just then we heard Jerry's voice call out, "You know the best way to attract bears at night? Make a lot of noise!"

That made the girls across the campsite laugh so hard that Rachel got up and turned on her flashlight. "What's all the racket about?" she asked them.

"Nothing."

"All right then. Time to get quiet."

All the flashlights went off, and the laughter stopped. I pulled my sleeping bag up under my chin and zipped it as far as it would go. I was nice and cozy this way, but a cool breeze was blowing that made my ears cold.

"I know Katherine's over there making fun of me," Laurel-Ann whispered. "I bet she told Brittany and Erin all kinds of mean things about me."

"I doubt that," I told her. "Anyway, they're quiet now, so don't worry about it."

I could hear Ashlin pulling her sleeping bag closer in the darkness. "Why do you think Katherine's making fun of you?" she asked.

"Because she hates me. Well, not just me. She hates everybody. She's so mean because she hates coming to Pine Haven every summer," said Laurel-Ann. "She calls it Pain Haven. And you want to know why she hates camp so much? The first year she came, she was only seven. She got dropped off, and then nobody came to pick her up. On the last day of camp, all the other campers left one by one, but nobody came to get Katherine."

Natasha made a gasping sound. "Oh my gosh! That's so sad!"

"Eda kept calling her parents, and nobody answered. So Katherine had to stay at camp for days and days after it was over, and nobody was here but Eda and all the counselors getting ready for the second session."

"What happened?" asked Ashlin. "Did somebody pick her up eventually?"

"Yeah, eventually. But it wasn't her parents. It was some relative or something. Now she doesn't live with her parents anymore. They're alive and everything, but they put her up for adoption when she was seven. Isn't that terrible?" Laurel-Ann was propped up on her elbows, whispering softly to us.

"Are you sure?" I asked. "That sounds pretty unbelievable."

"It's a true story! I swear! You want to know how I know?" asked Laurel-Ann. "Katherine told me herself. Last summer. She didn't always hate me so much. I thought maybe the two of us could be friends. But then she turned on me for no reason."

"Does it have something to do with Rainbow Trout?" I whispered.

"What's Rainbow Trout?" Natasha and Ashlin asked at the same time.

Suddenly a flashlight clicked on, and the beam was shining right in our eyes. "Oh, is that you girls talking?" We heard Rachel's voice through the darkness. "I thought we had a chipmunk invasion. All I could hear was chatter, chatter, chatter."

"We'll be quiet," Natasha told her.

And that was enough to make Laurel-Ann close her mouth.

Rainbow Trout. Rainbow Trout. I lay there in my sleeping bag, imagining all kinds of crazy stories. Did it have something to do with fish? Or rainbows? Or was it a code phrase of some kind?

I rolled over on the hard ground and glanced at Laurel-Ann's still form beside me. I doubted she'd ever tell me the story behind it. But she wasn't the only one who knew what it meant.

Katherine did too. Maybe she'd be willing to talk. I knew it was some big secret, but I was good at keeping secrets.

Most of the time.

CHAPTER 11

Tuesday, June 24

"What a quiet group," said Rachel, looking around at all of us. "I wonder what happened to the chatty bunch that was here last night?"

We were huddled around the campfire, only this morning there was no fire burning, just a pile of ashes and some dead embers. Breakfast was instant oatmeal and dried fruit, but it didn't taste as good as last night's dinner.

Nobody was talking much this morning because everybody was sore, cold, and tired from sleeping on the ground. When I'd first woken up, my sleeping bag was soaking wet with dew. Camping out was fun, but it did have its downsides.

As soon as breakfast was over, we had to get ready to leave. Jerry poured water on the already completely dead fire and spread out the embers with a stick, just to be safe.

"My back is killing me," Natasha groaned as she pulled on her backpack.

"I know. Mine too," I agreed.

"Can you believe that corny joke they played on us?" asked Ashlin. We'd woken up to find strands of red yarn hanging from lots of the tree branches. Lori insisted that the ghost of the redheaded woman had visited us during the night.

"I'm sure I heard her calling," she kept telling us. I'd liked the story, and I thought it was funny to find all that red yarn.

We fell into a long line in about the same spots we'd been in yesterday, with Laurel-Ann and me toward the back and Katherine far enough away not to bother her. Nobody was talking much, including Laurel-Ann.

Even though this morning's hike wasn't quite as much fun as yesterday's, I still tried to enjoy it. I noticed a couple of tiny mushrooms shooting up among the dead leaves on the ground. They were bright orange with long, slender stalks and little caps. I'd never seen anything like them before.

"I think everyone's half-asleep," Rachel called out

from the front of the line. "Let's make some sound!" Then she started singing the hiking song.

I was beginning to learn some of the camp songs, but there were so many, it was hard to keep up with all of them. This one was to the tune of "I've Been Working on the Railroad." Ahead of us, everyone else was singing, so I mumbled the parts I knew.

Come go hiking on some trails, girls, if you want some fun!
Hike these mountains every day, girls, in the wind or rain or sun.
Yes, you know adventure's waiting,
Backpacking, camping, and trailblazing.
Get your compass and your flashlight—
Let's go on a hike!
Hiking we will go, hiking we will go,
Hiking we will go today, today!
Hiking we will go, hiking we will go,
Hiking we will go today!

The trail was getting steeper now as it wound higher and higher through the trees. I wondered if everyone else was as tired as I was. We hiked on and on, and I kept thinking what a long hike it had been yesterday, which meant we had to go just as far today. Finally the hikers at the front of the line stopped.

"Anyone ready for a quick break?" Rachel shouted.

We all groaned with relief and slipped our backpacks off our aching shoulders. Laurel-Ann sat next to me on a flat rock. Everybody else sat on the ground or on a fallen log that was just off the trail. Sunshine was coming through the branches overhead and making a pattern of dancing light on the leaf-covered ground.

Rachel passed around a big bag of gorp, and we each scooped out a handful. I watched Laurel-Ann eat all the peanuts and raisins first and save the M&M's for last.

"Why is this stuff called gorp?" Natasha asked.

"I've heard it stands for 'good old raisins and peanuts,'" said Jerry from where he stood, leaning against a tree with his arms folded across his chest.

"But what about the M&M's? Maybe it should be called marp," Laurel-Ann suggested. Brittany let out a loud laugh, and everyone turned to look at her.

Katherine was sitting a few feet away with a book in her lap, and she was busy writing in it. Brittany and Erin were looking over her shoulder and laughing.

"What's so funny?" Ashlin asked them.

Brittany looked up with a little smile on her face. "Oh, nothing!" she said lightly.

Laurel-Ann motioned for Natasha and Ashlin to come over to where we were sitting. "That's what they were laughing about last night. I know she's writing something about me! I just know it!" Laurel-Ann whispered to the rest of us. "I wouldn't be surprised if she was writing something about all of us."

"It could be anything," said Natasha. "I doubt it has anything to do with us."

"You don't know Katherine like I do! She's always saying mean things about people."

Laurel-Ann twisted the end of one braid nervously between her fingers. Then she looked at us, and her eyes got really big. "We've got to figure out some way to get it and see what they're saying about us."

"Okay, break's over!" Rachel announced. Everyone stood up and put on their backpacks again.

"Why don't we just ask them to let us see the book?" Ashlin suggested.

"I think we should just forget about the whole thing," said Natasha. She took off her glasses and rubbed the lenses on her T-shirt before putting them on again.

"But don't you want to know what it says?"

"I'm a little curious," I admitted as we fell into single file again and started down the trail. But I was a lot more curious about what Rainbow Trout meant. Who knew what they were writing in the book? It could be anything.

Something funny, obviously. But that didn't necessarily mean it was about all of us. Or even about Laurel-Ann. I doubted that Erin and Brittany would be like that. They'd both been really nice to me.

"We've just got to get our hands on that book!" Laurel-Ann whispered to me.

"How?" I asked.

Then she spent the next ten minutes making all these crazy plans to cause a distraction the next time we stopped to take a break, so that we could secretly switch backpacks with Katherine and then read the book when no one was looking.

"I honestly don't think that's going to work," I tried to tell her.

From the front of the line, we could hear lots of laughter again. It was Brittany, because by now I recognized her laugh. But also Jerry. And sometimes Rachel and Lori.

"What's going on up there?" I asked Natasha and Ashlin, who were in front of us.

"I'm not sure," said Natasha. She and Ashlin slowed down a little so that we could catch up with them on the trail.

"I think they're teasing Jerry, asking him if he'll ever get married," Ashlin explained. "I heard them asking him if he'd make his wife camp out on their honeymoon, and he said, 'What other kind of vacation is there?'"

More and more laughter. Whatever they were talking about sure was cracking them all up. I had to admit that it was a little annoying always being on the outside of the joke. It would've been nice if they could've let the rest of us in on it.

"Do you think Katherine's up there making fun of us?" Laurel-Ann asked me.

I let out a tired sigh. "Honestly, Laurel-Ann, I don't. They're talking about Jerry." I wanted to remind her that not everything was about her, but I didn't want to sound annoyed with her. Even though I was. She really was kind of paranoid.

I looked up to see Katherine standing off to the side of the trail. She seemed absolutely furious about something. Her face was bright red, and her teeth were clenched. She looked like a firecracker about to explode.

"Are you okay?" asked Natasha as she and Ashlin got close to her.

Katherine didn't answer her. She stood there breathing heavily in and out, staring at a spot on the ground.

Ashlin and Natasha watch her curiously as they walked past, and then they looked back at Laurel-Ann and me with surprised expressions. I could tell Laurel-Ann didn't even want to go near Katherine, but we were about to pass her on the trail.

Katherine didn't so much as blink when we went by. She just kept staring at the ground and frowning. Her chest was heaving up and down.

I looked over my shoulder to see what she was going to do. She was still standing there, and now we were all walking away from her.

"What was that all about?" asked Ashlin, looking back at Katherine, who hadn't moved from her spot.

"I have no idea," I answered.

"I bet I know!" Laurel-Ann said suddenly. "I bet she's mad because they're all teasing Jerry about his future wife! Didn't you notice how yesterday she was constantly following him? 'Oh Jerry, I'll help you get firewood. Jerry, what's the name of that tree? Jerry, what's the longest hike you've ever been on?'" she said in a singsongy voice.

"Hey, you guys," I said, looking back. "She still hasn't moved. Maybe we should tell someone. We can't just leave her behind."

Now we couldn't even see her behind us anymore. I didn't want the whole group to get so far away from her that she couldn't catch up with us. "I think I'll go check on her," I told them. Ashlin called out to the front of the group for the others to stop for a minute.

I turned and hurried back down the trail to where Katherine was. She hadn't moved. Her long, tangled hair was hanging in her eyes, and her face was still flushed.

"Katherine, is everything all right?" I asked.

She shifted her eyes in my direction and then looked at the ground. "Go away!"

"Um, everyone is waiting for us. Maybe we should keep walking and catch up with them," I suggested.

"Why don't you leave me alone?" she snapped at me.

I turned and walked a few feet away from her. "I know you're upset. But I'm staying with you till you feel better." I was about to take a seat on the trail when she suddenly started moving.

"Fine! I'm coming!" she bellowed. "I don't know what the big deal is. If I got lost, no one would even notice."

We were both walking up the trail now. Katherine made a point of walking far behind me, but at least we were moving again. Pretty soon we were back at the end of the line of hikers.

"Everything all right back there?" Jerry yelled to us. I could just see his face over the heads of everyone else in line.

"Yep, everything's fine," I shouted. Laurel-Ann glared at me, but I just shrugged a little and hung back from the other hikers so that Katherine could keep up with me.

She was intentionally walking very slowly. I had to admit, there were times when I felt like just walking away and leaving her, but I forced myself to slow down too. I had no idea what she was so mad about. Maybe Laurel-Ann had been right. Maybe she was upset that Brittany and the others were taking up Jerry's attention now, but whatever was wrong, I felt sorry for her.

She seemed like such an unhappy person. And I could relate to that—all these girls around you having a great time when the only thing you could think about was that you'd rather be somewhere else.

Katherine had stopped to pick up a walking stick, and I could hear her back there slashing at all the stray branches and leaves along the path. It sounded like she was blazing her own trail instead of bringing up the rear of the one we were on.

I stopped for a second when I noticed a beautiful sight. We'd come to a spot in the trail where there was one lone mushroom poking up through the dead leaves. Unlike the little orange ones I kept seeing, this one had a thick stalk and a wide, flat crown, and it was a deep shade of purple.

"Oh, cool," I gasped, bending down to look at it. I really wished I'd brought my camera along. It was so perfect. I stood up slowly and walked away from it.

And then I heard a stomp. When I looked around, I saw Katherine standing right over the spot where the mushroom had been. She had an evil grin on her face, and she slowly raised her muddy sneaker up to show me the squashed mushroom underneath. She was staring right at me, daring me with her eyes to say something.

I stood there in absolute shock. "Why did you do that? I tried to be nice to you, and that's the way you treat me?"

Katherine's face changed. Her eyes dropped down to the squashed mushroom, and she didn't look at me again. "Sorry."

I turned away and kept walking. We fell back into our pattern of bringing up the rear of the line, with the two of us so far behind the others that at times we almost couldn't see them.

We'd been walking that way in complete silence for at least ten minutes when Katherine called out to me. "Kayla? Here's another purple one."

Up until that moment, I hadn't even realized that she knew my name. I turned around to see Katherine pointing with her walking stick to a bright purple mushroom growing just off the trail. Was she getting my attention so she could whack it with her stick? I waited and watched, but she just stood there pointing to it.

"They're so pretty," I said finally. "And the little orange ones, too."

"Yeah," Katherine agreed, still staring at it. "Sorry about the other one."

"It's okay."

We kept walking, the two of us far behind the others. That's how we spent the rest of the hike. Birds flying over our heads must have seen a funny sight. A line of people all pretty close together, followed by one straggler, followed by a second straggler.

When we finally reached camp, Katherine didn't say anything to me as she walked away, but she did give me a faint smile.

Laurel-Ann came up to me with a worried look on

her face. "Kayla, are you mad at me for some reason?" she asked.

"No! Of course not! Why would I be mad at you?" I asked.

"How come you just left me and spent the rest of the hike with her?"

I shrugged. "I don't know. Something was wrong with her. Somebody needed to make sure she didn't just stay in the woods while we hiked off and left her. I guess I feel sorry for her," I tried to explain.

"Did you talk to her? Are you friends with her now?" Laurel-Ann looked completely panicked. She grabbed my arm and squeezed it. "Did she tell you what Rainbow Trout means?"

"No, we hardly said more than three words to each other. All I did was slow down so she wasn't left behind." We were dragging ourselves slowly up the hill on our way to the cabin. My sweatshirt was hot and sticky, and it smelled like the smoke from last night's fire. I couldn't wait to get this backpack off and take a hot shower. I also wanted to find out from Shelby if anything else had happened with Boo.

"Well, if she ever does tell you the Rainbow Trout story, I just want you to know it's a lie." She'd finally stopped squeezing my arm.

"Really?" I asked. "If you told me it first, the true story, then I'd know for sure Katherine was lying." I glanced at her quickly. "I swear I'll keep it a secret."

Laurel-Ann let out a loud sigh. "I know you would. I trust you." She shook her head back and forth. "But I don't want to talk about it." And by the way she kept her mouth closed, I could tell she meant it.

CHAPTER 12

Friday, June 27

"So all we have to do is wait until a time when we know her cabin will be empty, like during activities. Then we just go inside and find Katherine's trunk. That part will be easy, because I know what hers looks like from last year. It's red, and there's lots of peeling-off stickers all over the top of it. And then we'll just open her trunk and see if we can find it."

Laurel-Ann was describing the elaborate plan of how we should go about finding the book. Earlier today, a big group of us had gone on a hike to Lookout Point, and Katherine had come along. She'd teased Laurel-Ann as usual, calling her Rainbow Trout, and that had started Laurel-Ann worrying about the book again.

It had just been a day hike, and Katherine hadn't brought her book along, but seeing her again was enough to remind Laurel-Ann about it. She was absolutely convinced that this mysterious book had all kinds of horrible things about her inside it.

"It sounds like breaking and entering to me," I told her. It was late in the afternoon, and activities were over now, so that meant free time was starting. We were walking back from the tennis courts, and I wanted so badly to have this time alone so I could visit Samantha and then get my practice time in. But Laurel-Ann was stuck to me like one of those prickly burrs that I was always pulling off my socks any time I came back from hiking in the woods.

Laurel-Ann smacked the strings of her tennis racket against her palm. "No, we're not breaking into anything. I know you think it's snooping, but maybe it's not even in her trunk. It might be out on a shelf in plain sight, and then we could just take a quick look inside to see what they've said about us."

"Listen, you're never going to convince me to go into Katherine's cabin and look for that book."

"Well, how are we ever going to find out what they said about us otherwise?"

"Why don't you just forget about it?" I suggested.

"That was days ago. I can't believe you're still so obsessed about this."

"I'm not obsessed, it's just that . . ." She stopped talking and glanced around. "Where are we going?" she asked, because we were heading in the direction of Junior Line.

"Well, I'm going to see my little sister," I said. "I haven't had a chance to talk to her in a couple of days." I handed my tennis racket to Laurel-Ann. "Would you mind taking this back to the cabin for me? I'll see you at dinner, okay?"

Laurel-Ann took the hint. And she also took my racket. "Okay. I'll save you a seat beside me if I get there first!"

I let out a relieved sigh. That was one way to get rid of her.

Unfortunately, Samantha wasn't in her cabin, and her friend Mary Claire, who was in there by herself, didn't seem to know where I could find her.

So I went straight to the lodge. I didn't have my sheet music with me, and I didn't want to risk going back to the cabin and seeing Laurel-Ann again, so I would just work on scales and pieces that I had memorized instead.

I was surprised to walk into the lodge and see Shelby

sitting on the piano bench. "Hey, I've been waiting for you. I thought you might show up here pretty soon."

She had her swimsuit on, and a towel was wrapped around her waist like a long skirt. "Are you going to the lake?" I asked.

"Yeah, some of us from the Guard Start class need to work on service hours. But I wanted to give you an update first. Without Bubonic around."

She scooted over on the bench so I could sit down. "What's the latest?" I asked.

Shelby grinned. "I left the third note in her mailbox today. This one said, 'Bubonic Boo, we're watching your every move. Don't be responsible for Pine Haven's next outbreak.'"

This week it seemed like the rumors had definitely slowed down a lot, if not stopped completely. None of us had heard any new rumors about ourselves, or anyone else for that matter. I wasn't sure if Shelby's little anonymous notes to Boo were responsible or not. I didn't really care, just so long as she'd stopped talking about us.

"You know it's driving her crazy!" I said, softly fingering the notes of an A scale. "You're sure she's getting them? And she doesn't suspect who's doing it?"

"She's getting them, all right." Shelby chuckled.

"Whenever I leave a note in her mailbox, I always watch her after lunch to see her reaction. Today she read the note and then wadded it up and threw it in the trash can on the dining hall porch. But you should've seen how red her face was! She has no idea who's leaving the notes."

"It does seem to be helping," I admitted. "She's stopped talking about us. At least for now."

"Yeah." Shelby plucked out a few notes of "Chopsticks." "Hey, I better go. Just wanted to keep you in the loop."

I was glad to have this alone time now. Today I wanted to work on Chopin's Prelude in E Minor. The hardest thing for me about this piece was to remember not to rush through it. The pedal parts were really important, and since the soft pedal on this piano was out, that made it tougher, but I tried to not stress about it.

I reminded myself that it could be worse. I could not have any piano at all to practice on.

I'd been playing for about twenty minutes when I heard someone cough behind me, the kind of cough people make when they want to be noticed. I turned around and saw Katherine standing in the door.

"Oh, hi," I said. It sort of got on my nerves the way people would come in and listen to me while I was practicing. But there seemed to be something about the sound of a piano playing that just made people want to come near it.

Katherine and I hadn't really talked on the hike today since Laurel-Ann was around, but she did give me a tiny, almost unnoticeable smile. I guess I'd made a few points with her from the overnight when we'd hiked back together.

"I heard somebody in here playing," said Katherine. "I thought it was you. You come in here a lot, don't you?"

"I try to practice every day if I can." I had turned slowly around again and was fingering the keys softly.

"You play really well. Is it hard?" She was now standing right behind me.

"No, not really hard, but it does take a lot of time. You don't learn everything at once. I've been taking lessons since I was eight," I told her.

"Wow. No wonder you're so good. I'd never be able to play the piano." Katherine had on a stained, baggy T-shirt. I wondered if the girls in her cabin teased her about her clothes.

"Of course you could. You want to sit down?" I suggested, scooting to one end of the bench. "I'll show you some stuff."

She looked really surprised by my offer, but she sat

down on the bench next to me. She held her hands over the keyboard without touching the keys. "What do I do first?" she asked nervously.

"Well, see this note beside these two black keys? That's middle C." I played it so she could hear the tone. "Then here's D, E, F, G, A, B, and we're back to C again. That makes an octave."

I showed her how to play a C scale because it was the easiest, and how to use five fingers instead of just her index finger, the way most beginners usually started out.

"Wow, that's easy," said Katherine, after she'd played the scale several times.

"See? Here, I'll show you a really easy song to play as a duet. Do you know 'Heart and Soul'?" I asked.

She shook her head, so I played it for her.

"That doesn't look easy. I could never play that."

"Sure you can. Here's the right-hand part." I plucked out the tune for her with one finger. "See? It's not very different from playing a C scale. Now you try it."

Katherine tucked her long hair behind both ears and tried to play what I'd just showed her. She needed a little help to find C again after G, but after a couple of tries, she had it down.

"Easy, right?" I asked. "Now while you're playing the

treble part, I'll play the bass, the left-hand part. I'll nod when it's time for you to come in." I started off, playing it slowly but with some bounce, and then she came in right on cue.

When we finished playing, Katherine had a huge grin on her face. "That sounded really good! I can't believe I know how to play something!"

"Here, let's switch places, and I'll show you how to play the left-hand part."

"Oh, no way. I can't play that. It's way too hard," she said.

"No, it's not really. Just try it."

I showed her how to make the chords with three fingers, but she was getting a little frustrated with that, so I told her to just use two fingers instead. The left-hand part was more challenging for a beginner, and she messed up on it quite a bit, but I liked the way she was concentrating so hard, trying to get it down.

"Wait," she'd say whenever she made a mistake, and she tried it over and over again till she got it right.

"That's good. You're persistent," I told her. "A lot of beginners give up too easily if it's hard for them."

Katherine smiled, but she kept her eyes focused on the keyboard. She seemed so determined to play it well.

"There," I said, after she'd spent a good ten minutes

working on the left-hand part. "Now you know how to play a song."

Katherine was resting her fingers on the keyboard. "I love this," she said quietly. She said it so seriously that I couldn't keep from smiling.

"Maybe you can take lessons," I suggested.

Katherine shook her head and stared at the keyboard. "That's never going to happen. I live with my aunt."

"Oh." I wasn't sure what else to say to that.

"She's kind of young, so it's not like there's a lot of extra money for stuff like piano lessons," said Katherine.

Her voice sounded so sad. I waited to see if she'd say anything else.

"And who knows how long I'll be living with her? I've been there since last summer. Before that, I lived with a different aunt and uncle, and before that, I lived with my grandparents. I was with them from the time I was seven until I was ten. But then my grandpa got really sick, so I couldn't live with them anymore. They're the ones who pay for me to come to Pain Haven every summer."

I was shocked to hear all this. Suddenly I remembered Laurel-Ann's story about Katherine being put up for adoption by her parents. I'd thought it was a crazy rumor like so many things I'd heard this summer. But it was sort of true. I wondered about the story of her being left at camp for days when she was only seven. Was there any truth to that?

"I move around a lot too," I said. "I've lived in three different states. We're actually moving right now. When my sister and I left for camp, we were still in Maryland, but when camp ends we'll go to our new house in Florida. I haven't even seen it yet." My voice cracked a little when I said that.

"Sounds like you're pretty depressed about having to move," she said, looking at me for the first time since we started talking.

I just nodded and looked down at the keyboard. Why was I suddenly so sad talking about this?

Maybe because today I'd gotten a letter from Danielle. It was the third one she'd written me so far, which was great. I loved getting mail. Only there was a problem: I hadn't written her yet, and she was really starting to wonder why. I hadn't written to Maricela either. Or Emily.

Actually, I hadn't written a single letter so far to any of my friends. I knew it was rude not to, because I'd told all of them I would, but for some reason, I just couldn't make myself write to them.

Maybe I wasn't being rude. Just realistic. What was

the point of keeping up a bunch of long-distance friendships? Everybody else in the cabin was always writing letters, but it wasn't the same for me. They were all writing to people they knew they'd see again in a few weeks. But when was I ever going back to Maryland? Not anytime soon, that was for sure.

"You live with your parents, though, right?" asked Katherine.

"Of course," I answered. And then I wished I could take it back, because it sounded like I was saying, *Who doesn't live with their parents?* "I mean, yeah. I do."

"I'm glad I don't live with my parents. They're so screwed up." Katherine very gently fingered the right-hand part to "Heart and Soul." "My dad's divorced from his third wife. I have four stepbrothers and sisters. He doesn't take care of any of them, either. And my mom? Who knows where she's living right now? Or if she has a job or some new boyfriend. She calls me every now and then and says she'll come get me soon when she gets settled down. But she's not the kind of person who ever settles down." Katherine shook her head and suddenly banged on the keys with both hands.

Wow. I couldn't believe how bad Katherine really had it. And here I was, feeling sorry for myself because we had to move. At least I had two great parents. I had nothing to complain about.

"Do you get along with your aunt?" I asked. I was almost afraid to hear her answer.

"Yeah, I do. She's funny, and she likes to cook, so we're always making brownies or cookies or trying some new recipe. But I liked it at my grandparents' best. I loved their old house. It had two stories, and a screened-in porch out back and a big yard. They had to sell it when Papa got sick. But the apartment my aunt lives in has a pool." Katherine let out a deep sigh. "My aunt has a new boyfriend, though. If she gets married, I don't know where I'll end up."

I stared straight ahead. My eyes had that hot feeling, like the tears were about to start flowing any second. The thing was, I wasn't sure who I felt like crying for— Katherine or me.

I blinked hard and cleared my throat. "Want me to teach you another song?" I asked her.

"Yeah, I do," Katherine answered. "Something cheerful. I think we could both use it."

CHAPTER 13

Monday, June 30

"You two are becoming regular trailblazers," said Gloria as she watched Laurel-Ann and me packing our back-packs. It was late afternoon, and we were in the cabin getting our stuff ready for tonight's trip.

"Oh, we won't be trailblazing on this hike," said Laurel-Ann, stuffing a pair of jeans into her backpack. "This is a night hike, so it's totally different from trailblazing, where you go off into the wilderness and mark out your own trail. And that's fun too, but the point of this hike is to try to spot nocturnal wildlife, and now we'll be—"

"Uh, yeah, I guess I didn't mean 'trailblazing,'" Gloria said with a little laugh. "I just meant, you know, that you and Kayla are becoming great outdoor adventurers these days." Gloria smiled at me with a twinkly look in her eye. I could tell she was thinking, *Good luck trying to keep Laurel-Ann quiet while you observe wildlife.*

"We'd better go," I said, pulling on my backpack.

"Have fun," Shelby told us.

"Thanks," I said.

"Watch out for bears," Boo called out as we left the cabin.

Boo might have gotten better about not spreading rumors, but now she seemed to have a different hobby. Somebody in our cabin was playing pranks on all the Side A girls, one by one. At first we thought it was Devon and Maggie pranking each other, because they were the first ones to get them. But then someone played a prank on Betsy, so now the Side A girls were pointing fingers at us.

But mostly at Boo. She denied it, of course, but I just didn't trust that girl.

As we walked to the meeting spot for the hikers, Laurel-Ann talked on and on about how much fun she and I were going to have on this trip. It wasn't going to be just any old hike, either. We were leaving late in the day so we could set up camp before dark, and then we'd go out on a hike by moonlight. Without flashlights. How cool was that?

"Good to see all you regulars," announced Jerry when we got to the hiking storage shed. Brittany and Erin were already here, and Katherine was right by Jerry's side. She smiled when she saw me. "Hey, Kayla."

"Hi," I said, smiling back at her. It was nice to see Katherine looking almost cheerful for a change, but her happy mood seemed to set Laurel-Ann on edge. She scooted so close to me, I thought we'd both have to wear the same backpack.

"Are Ashlin and Natasha coming on this trip?" Laurel-Ann asked Rachel.

"I think so. This crew seems to be the only ones willing to sleep out on the ground all night," said Rachel. "It looks like we're going to have the same bunch."

When Natasha and Ashlin showed up a few minutes later, we were ready to leave.

"I have some bad news, and I know a lot of you are going to be disappointed," Rachel announced as we fell into line.

"What?" asked Erin. She sounded concerned.

"It's a really short hike to our campout spot," said Rachel, hanging her head, as if she'd just told us the worst news in the world.

"Oh, ha ha! Thanks for scaring us!" yelled Ashlin.

It really didn't take us long at all to get to the place

where we were setting up camp. And the scenery here was very different from where we'd been last time. We were in an open meadow with tall grass. There were some trees around the edges of the field, but otherwise it was nothing like our first overnight spot.

"Okay, we're not lighting a fire tonight because we don't want to scare any animals away with the smell of the smoke," Jerry told us. "But we still need some volunteers who are willing and able to take on a really big responsibility."

Katherine raised her hand immediately, and so did Laurel-Ann and Ashlin.

"I don't know if I can handle a lot of responsibility," said Brittany suspiciously.

Jerry doubled over with laughter. "I admire your honesty. The rest of you—do you know you just volunteered to dig the latrine?"

"Boy, you guys are a bunch of comedians tonight," Ashlin groaned.

Jerry just laughed. He put his hand on Katherine's head and ruffled up her hair. "Katherine volunteers for everything. She and I dug the latrine last time, so tonight you two can have the honors." He handed Ashlin the shovel. "Take turns so you won't get blisters."

Laurel-Ann gave me a sad look as she walked away

with Ashlin to the small grove of trees at the edge of the field.

Jerry, Rachel, and Lori were busy unpacking the tarps and spreading them out, so the rest of us helped them out. The sun had already set, but it was still light outside. The sky had faded into a pale, pearly color with a little pink still glowing just above the horizon.

"Did you see that look on Rainbow Trout's face? Wasn't that hilarious?" asked Katherine when the two of us were spreading out one of the tarps.

"Yeah. She didn't look very thrilled, did she?" I agreed.

I couldn't believe it! This was my chance. I'd been waiting for a moment when Katherine and I were alone, and when we weren't both talking about sad family stories. Laurel-Ann was gone. Katherine herself had just brought it up. The timing couldn't be more perfect.

"By the way, why do you always call her Rainbow Trout?" I asked. I hoped I sounded very casual about the whole thing and not like I was about to die of curiosity. Although I was.

Katherine started laughing. "She didn't tell you?" she asked. "She didn't tell you the famous Rainbow Trout story?"

I shook my head. "All she would say was that it

happened last summer, and she doesn't want to talk about it." I untied the ties on my sleeping bag and rolled it out on top of the tarp.

"Don't worry. I'll tell you the whole thing. It doesn't surprise me she wouldn't want you to know. Last summer, Laurel-Ann and I were actually friends, if you can believe it," Katherine started off.

What I couldn't believe was that I was finally going to hear this story.

"We were in the same cabin, and we did lots of stuff together, and she was really nice to me. But then something happened that changed all that."

Suddenly there was a loud scream. It scared me so much I thought my heart was going to stop. "Snake! Snake! Snake!" Brittany shrieked. She had jumped backward about three feet off the ground.

"Calm down!" Rachel told her, leaning over to look deep into the grass where Brittany was pointing. "Oh, that? It's just a little garter snake."

Rachel bent down and stood up again. We all stepped back, because she had a long, wiggling snake by its head. Erin and Natasha ran over to see what was going on.

"Oh my gosh!" I gasped. I couldn't believe she was standing there so calmly with a snake in her hand. It made me shudder just looking at how it wrapped itself around her bare arm.

Jerry and Lori walked up behind her. "Oh, yeah. That won't hurt anybody," said Jerry. "Little green fellow like that. Rattlesnakes, water moccasins, coral snakes, and copperheads. Those are the ones you need to stay away from."

"Anybody else want to hold it?" asked Rachel. She held the snake's head still between her thumb and forefinger.

The snake had black beady eyes and a little red tongue that darted in and out, but now that we got a closer look, it really didn't look quite so scary. Its body was bright green and about as thick as my little finger.

Brittany had calmed down now. She was even smiling over the way Rachel was holding the snake up to show us all. She went over to Katherine and gave her a nudge. "You've got to draw a picture of that," she whispered to her. "Rachel, the Amazing Snake Handler."

Katherine smiled at her. "Let's get the book."

Even though Katherine seemed to have forgotten the Rainbow Trout story for the moment, my ears perked up when I heard them mention the book. Laurel-Ann had no idea what she was missing.

Rachel took the little snake over to a spot away from

our campsite. Everyone else was still busy unfolding the tarps and rolling out sleeping bags.

I followed Brittany and Katherine as they went over to where the backpacks were lined up in the grass. They all looked basically the same, and they had to unzip a few before they found Katherine's book.

"We were wondering what you were writing in there," I said. "What was so funny?"

I couldn't believe how calm I sounded. Here they were, right in front of me, holding this mysterious book that Laurel-Ann had spent so much time worrying about. And neither one of them seemed to care that I was with them.

"Oh, that's right. Your group didn't see it last time, did you?" said Katherine. "Here, take a look." And just like that, she handed it to me. I stood there, holding it in my hands. The book. I was actually going to get a chance to see inside Katherine's book.

The cover was pink with yellow flowers, and across the front it said, "Happy Memories." I opened it up slowly and flipped through the pages while my heart ticked away like a metronome set at 180. Definitely a presto tempo.

There was some writing inside, but mostly there were drawings. I looked at page after page. Lots of drawings were of a man who was obviously Jerry—hiking with a backpack, standing on top of a mountain. All the pictures had funny captions.

I turned the pages to some other drawings. One picture was of our last campfire circle, with all of us sitting around it. A girl with braids was holding up a flaming marshmallow on a stick. The balloon caption coming out of her mouth said, "Is this overdone?"

Then there were drawings of Rachel and Lori. Rachel had a big smile on her face and was asking, "Do I smell wild honeysuckle?" Lori had a surprised look. "No, that's my new deodorant," her balloon caption read.

A few pages had writing on them. Across the top, someone had written different questions. "What do you like best about Pine Haven?" and below it were answers. "Nothing." "Being with my friends." "Going on campouts and eating s'mores!"

"What do you like best about this campout?" another question asked. "Listening to Jerry's hiking stories." "S'mores!!" "Listening to ghost stories."

I turned the page. "Do you think Rachel and Jerry would make a cute couple?" "NO!" "Yes, they do!" "Sort of. But I don't think he's the romantic type!"

"Do you think Jerry's cute?" "YES!" "Eww! He's

sorta old, don't you think??" "He looks good for his age, though."

"Oh, don't read that stuff!" said Brittany, looking over my shoulder. "We were just being silly." She reached for the book, and I handed it back to her.

So that was all there was to it! Nothing about any of us!

I felt so relieved. "Funny drawings," I commented. "Who's the artist?"

"Katherine," said Brittany. "She's good, isn't she?"

"Hey, everyone. We should eat before it gets dark," Rachel called out to us. "Come get your sack suppers."

"Do you mean we're having peanut butter and honey sandwiches?" Erin asked.

"Yeah, doesn't that sound yummy?" said Rachel, throwing one arm around her shoulder and giving her a big squeeze.

Ashlin and Laurel-Ann came walking back, looking very dusty. Everyone had sat down in a big circle with their sacks, and there was a lot of grumbling over how these sandwiches couldn't compare to the campfire stew we'd had last time, but Jerry and Rachel took our minds off that by talking about our upcoming nighttime adventure.

"I have to tell you something," I whispered to Laurel-

Ann. "After we finish eating, act like we're going to the latrine, okay?" She looked at me and nodded solemnly. Katherine was sitting across the circle from us, next to Jerry and Lori. She was totally focused on everything Jerry was saying, but I still didn't want to talk about the book in front of her.

As soon as we'd finished and gathered our trash, Laurel-Ann and I walked away together in the direction of the latrine.

Once we were far enough away from the group, I made my announcement. "You're never going to believe what I saw when you were gone. I saw the book!"

Laurel-Ann sucked in her breath. "You did? What did Katherine say about me?" She grabbed my arm and squeezed it so tight that the circulation was cut off.

"It didn't say anything! Honestly! It was mostly funny pictures that Katherine had drawn."

"Were there any of me?" asked Laurel-Ann. In the fading light, I could barely see her face, but I could hear the worried tone of her voice.

"Only one. With your marshmallow on fire." I described that picture and all the others I'd seen, along with the pages that had the different questions and comments. "Really, there was nothing bad in there at all. That's what they were laughing about last time—

just all those cartoons. Did you know she was such a good artist?"

"Are you sure? Are you positive there wasn't anything mean?" she asked.

"Yes, I am. I swear there's nothing bad in there at all. Trust me."

Laurel-Ann slowly released the grip she had on my arm. "Okay. I guess that's good news, huh?" she asked, as if she wasn't exactly convinced.

"Of course. Now let's go back with the others and try to enjoy this overnight."

What a relief. The book had turned out to be nothing, and now Laurel-Ann would stop worrying about it. The hike by moonlight to look for wildlife was going to be amazing! But the best thing about the whole night was that there wasn't going to be any more drama.

CHAPTER 14

When we got back to the campsite, Jerry and Rachel broke us up into two groups. "It'll be easier for us to stay quiet that way. Remember, no talking. And no sudden movements if you do see anything," Rachel instructed.

Natasha, Ashlin, Laurel-Ann, and I were in Rachel's group, and Jerry took Katherine, Brittany, Erin, and Lori in his group. We separated and went off in opposite directions across the meadow. It was now completely dark, but with a full moon out tonight, it was bright enough for us to see pretty easily. Rachel led the way, and she walked so slowly and quietly that the rest of us did the same thing.

When we came to a spot near some trees, we sat

down in the grass and waited. No one said a word, not even Laurel-Ann. I couldn't help thinking about how hard that must be for her, and I almost started to giggle.

I was amazed by how bright it really was in the moonlight. The grass of the meadow looked silvery, and every time the wind blew, it shimmered in the breeze. Since my eyes were used to being outside now, I could easily see everyone's face.

Natasha spotted something first. She nudged me because I was sitting beside her, and then she pointed toward the trees. Two dark forms moved across the ground.

Raccoons! Two raccoons had just climbed down from a tree and were now waddling out into view! We all exchanged excited looks. I could see Rachel's big grin. None of us moved a muscle.

The raccoons didn't seem to notice us. They scratched around in the grass, foraging for something. Their little white masks and black bandit eyes were very clear in the moonlight. I wished so badly for a camera. But the flash would've scared them away. So I sat still and stared, printing the image of them onto my memory.

We watched them for the longest time. They were just going about their business, looking for insects and anything else they could find. Eventually they moved far enough away so that we couldn't see them anymore.

"That was amazing!" said Ashlin. "They were so adorable!"

"I know!" I agreed. We whispered excitedly about it until Rachel shushed us.

After that, not much happened. We waited and watched, but there wasn't anything to see. At least not any animals. But I still liked leaning back on my elbows and gazing up at the night sky. There were so many stars, and I could easily spot the Big Dipper and Little Dipper. The moon looked like a huge white orange hovering in the sky.

It was about that time that the deer came into view. Rachel got our attention, and then we saw several of them crossing the meadow. One, two—I counted five, I thought. Maybe six. It was hard to tell because they were moving in a group, staying close together. We were all so quiet that we could hear them rustling the grass as they moved. They would stop and hold their heads up, constantly on the lookout. Then they nibbled at the grass before moving on to another spot.

This was the most incredible night! It was so much fun to be out here in the moonlight, seeing animals in their natural habitat. We didn't see anything else after that, but we were all so thrilled that we'd spotted both the raccoons and the deer.

When we met up with Jerry's group back at the campsite later, they'd had some encounters of their own. "We saw a skunk!" Brittany told us.

"Are you kidding? A skunk?" I asked.

"Yes! We were so scared it was going to squirt us, but we all kept really still."

They'd also seen the deer, but they hadn't seen our raccoons. Jerry had seen a possum in a tree, but nobody else did, so they thought maybe he was teasing them.

"Jerry, are there bears around this part of North Carolina?" asked Katherine.

"Yeah, there sure are. Black bears. Why do you think we're so careful with the food and always hang it from a tree branch?" he said.

"Think we'll see a bear tonight?" asked Natasha. She glanced around nervously.

"Not if y'all make as much noise as you did the last time. We should be safe."

After that, Rachel said it would be okay for us to tell ghost stories, so we got out flashlights and stretched out on our sleeping bags. We'd laid them out close together this time, not like last time, when we were in two separate groups. Katherine's book was getting passed around so that everyone had a chance to see her drawings.

Laurel-Ann had just finished looking at the book when she passed it to me.

"Did you see these? They're so funny. I didn't even mind the picture of me with the flaming marshmallow! And I'm glad I got to see the picture of Rachel, the Amazing Snake Handler, since I missed the real thing."

"Oh, I haven't seen the new drawings yet," I said, taking the book from her.

I clicked on my flashlight and opened up the book, but then I realized I had it upside down. I turned it over and started reading.

"What do you think of Natasha?" "Do you mean El Shrimpo?" "She's not a shrimp, she's a mouse." "Yeah, she acts like one too. Somebody should step on her."

All around me, everyone was talking and laughing, but my eyes were glued to the words on the page. What was this? I flipped through the book and realized that all the pages I'd seen earlier were at the front.

Then there were lots of blank pages, which made you think you'd come to the end of all the writing and drawings. But then—then there were several pages near the very back of the book where there was more writing.

"What do you think of Ashlin?" "His parents should have sent him to Camp Crockett!" "I know! What a bad haircut!" "Looks just like a boy!"

I swallowed hard as I turned the next page. "What do you think of Laurel-Ann?"

"You mean the Mouth that swallowed Pine Haven?" "Ha! Exactly! She never shuts up!!" "She has no real friends. What a loser."

My heart was tapping out staccato beats in my chest as I turned the page one more time. The last page had this question scrawled across the top. "What do you think of Kayla?" "Snobby rich girl." "Very unfriendly. Thinks she's better than everyone else." "My cat can play better piano than she can!"

I turned the page and there was nothing after that, just a few more blank pages at the end of the book.

But it didn't matter. I'd seen enough. I closed the book without saying a word.

CHAPTER 15

I had no idea what time it was when I crawled out of my sleeping bag. I only knew that it was the middle of the night. I'd been lying awake for the longest time, listening to the sounds of everyone else sleeping around me.

I had to get out of there. I had to get away, because I felt like I was made of glass. And I was about to break into millions of pieces.

As soon as I was out of my warm sleeping bag, I started shivering, even though it was a warm night. I'd been sleeping in my clothes, like everyone else, and luckily, I'd left my shoes next to my sleeping bag, so I slipped them on and tiptoed away.

There were some trees nearby, and if I could just get over there, I could be away from everyone. I didn't care what wild animals I might see. The moon was still glowing so brightly that everything was clearly visible—the grass, the meadow all around me, and the shadows of the trees off in the distance.

It could be worse. It could be worse. I tried to think of something to remind myself that there were worse things than reading a bunch of terrible things that people had said about you.

But no matter how hard I tried, I couldn't think of anything.

There was nothing worse. Nothing.

As soon as I got to the trees, I burst into tears. I'd been holding them in so long. I sank down and sat on the ground, holding my head in my hands. My whole body was shaking as the tears came gushing out.

Was that what they thought of me? Were they only pretending to be nice to me? Snobby rich girl? Very unfriendly? And that comment about my piano playing. That was the one that hurt the most.

My tears felt so hot as I wiped them away. I was never going to stop crying. It felt like I could cry all night long. And tomorrow when the sun came up, I'd still be sitting here, sobbing. The way my heart felt right now, I was sure I was never, ever going to stop feeling this sad.

"Kayla? Is that you?"

It was just a whisper, but it scared me so badly that I literally jumped.

"Kayla, are you out here? It's me—Laurel-Ann."

I could see her moving slowly toward me through the trees. I'd been crying so hard that now I was making little whimpering sounds, which I couldn't seem to control.

"I'm right here," I said finally.

"What are you doing out here? Are you okay?" She looked like a silver spirit walking through the moonlight.

I tried to answer her, but my voice didn't work. So I just started crying again.

"I saw you leave, and I was worried about you out here by yourself." Laurel-Ann sat down beside me under the tree. Her face seemed to be almost glowing. "You're crying. What's wrong?"

Every time I tried to open my mouth to say something, words wouldn't come out. I just sat there with my head resting on my folded arms and my knees drawn up, bawling my eyes out.

"It's okay," Laurel-Ann said softly. I could feel her hand on my shoulder, and very gently she patted my back. That only made it worse, so I cried even harder.

"It's okay. It's okay," Laurel-Ann kept saying. For once in her life, she wasn't talking too much. She sat beside me quietly and waited for me to get control of myself.

"I—I s-saw something," I said finally. My voice was all jerky and sobby sounding. "In the book. Mean things. People had written re-re-really mean things." I could see the look of surprise on her face. "You were right!" I exclaimed, and then the sobs burst out of me again.

"What do you mean? What did you see?"

I wiped my teary face with both hands. "In the book, people had written these horrible comments. I didn't see them the first time Katherine and Brittany showed it to me." I let out a really loud sniffle. "But then later, after we'd gone out on our night hike, when we were all telling ghost stories and passing the book around, I saw something."

"What was it?'"

"Pages at the very back of the book. It said, 'What do you think of Kayla?' and then there were these really mean comments about me." I started crying again.

I told her all the things that I'd read in there, and how much it had hurt me to think that people were saying those things about me.

Laurel-Ann gasped when she heard what they'd written. "It really said that?"

"I know I wasn't very friendly at first. But there was a reason! We're moving. My first day of camp was my last day in my old house," I wailed. "And when camp is over, we'll be moving to a new house in a new state. I don't want to move! But we had to. It was for my mom's job. I hate that I have to change schools. I hate that I'm leaving all my friends behind. I don't want to move! I don't want to move!"

I cried and cried and cried, and the whole time, Laurel-Ann sat there beside me with her arm around my shoulders. I'd never said those words out loud. I had tried not to even think them. But now here they were, exploding out of me.

"I don't mean to be snobby. I really don't. It's not that I think I'm better than everybody else. It's just . . . what's the point? Why make friends that you'll just have to say good-bye to and then never see again?"

"I'm so sorry," said Laurel-Ann. "I had no idea that you were going through that right now. I've never had to move. I've lived in the same house my whole life."

I looked at her. "Is that the way people really see me around here? A snobby rich girl? Am I really that unfriendly?"

"No! Not at all! The only person who thinks that

about you is Katherine. It's her book. She's the one who wrote all those things."

I shook my head. "It wasn't just Katherine. There were different comments. I——I think Erin and Brittany wrote those things too."

Laurel-Ann stared at me. "Was there anything about me?"

I made a snuffling noise and nodded. "Yes. There were pages for all four of us—Natasha and Ashlin, too. With terrible things written about all of us."

Laurel-Ann's face looked so pale with her hair hanging down loose around it. "What did they say about me?" she asked.

"Just, you know, about how you talk so much." I didn't want to be the one to tell her what I'd read. A couple of sobs escaped me. "I just can't believe they would be so mean!"

Laurel-Ann shook her head. "I can believe it! That's how Katherine is. I know from experience how awful she can be." She was quiet for a minute, and then she looked at me.

"Do you want me to tell you what Rainbow Trout means?"

I couldn't stop sniffling. "Only if you want to," I said.

"I will, because I know I can trust you not to tell

everybody else. Here's what happened. Last summer Katherine and I were friends. But then she turned on me. I think it was because she doesn't really have a family. She seemed really jealous of me. Anyway, she got mad at me, and so she put a dead fish in my bed—down at the bottom so my feet would touch it when I got in."

"Where did she get a dead fish?" I wanted to know.

Laurel-Ann shrugged. "I guess from the lake. Anyway, it scared me so bad that I screamed, and everyone got up to see what was wrong. And Katherine just laughed. She wouldn't apologize, and it made the whole cabin smell like fish, and she teased me for the rest of the summer about what a fishy smell I had. She's still teasing me a whole year later! She just won't let it drop!"

So that was the Rainbow Trout story. I'd finally gotten to hear it.

"That is pretty mean," I told her. "I can't believe she put a dead fish in your bed."

"It was so disgusting! It was all slimy and cold and wet! You should've heard how loud I screamed. And every time she says 'Rainbow Trout' to me, it reminds me of it," said Laurel-Ann.

I remembered how Katherine had stomped on that pretty purple mushroom I'd stopped to look at. She was capable of being really horrible when she wanted to be. I wished I'd never taught her how to play "Heart and Soul."

"It doesn't surprise me that Katherine could be so mean," I admitted to Laurel-Ann. "But Brittany and Erin? How could they be that way too? They seem so nice."

Laurel-Ann let out a sigh. "Lots of people are nice to your face. But then they'll say really mean things about you behind your back." She looked at me. "But they're wrong about you, Kayla. You're not snobby, and you're not unfriendly. And I think you're a wonderful piano player."

I smiled and wiped the tears away. "You've never even heard me play."

"Yes, I have. A little bit when I was walking by the lodge. And I think it's great that you're so dedicated and you practice all the time. I always liked that about you. I'm sorry you have to move. That must be really hard. You have every right to be sad about it. I know I would be."

I couldn't believe it—Laurel-Ann who talked nonstop and never said anything worth hearing was suddenly saying all the right things.

"Maybe we should go back now," I suggested. I knew

it was really, really late, and after all that crying, I was actually feeling tired now.

"Are you sure you're okay?"

I nodded. "I feel a little better. I just needed to cry."

"I know," said Laurel-Ann. "I've never understood why people think it's so terrible to cry. I think it helps to cry when you're sad."

"It helps to talk to someone too," I admitted.

"You can always talk to me. About anything. Anytime you're feeling sad. You can wake me up in the middle of the night if you want. I won't mind."

"Thanks," I said. "I'm glad you followed me out here."

Laurel-Ann stood up and gave me a tight squeeze. "Of course! What are friends for?"

CHAPTER 16

Tuesday, July 1

"I can't believe it," said Natasha. "I just can't believe it."

"It's true. Kayla saw it last night. It's at the very back of Katherine's book. A different page for each one of us. With all these mean comments written about us." Laurel-Ann was whispering to Natasha and Ashlin, telling them about the discovery I'd made. We'd just finished rolling up all the sleeping bags and putting away the tarps, and we were getting ready to hike back to Pine Haven.

"You actually saw it?" Ashlin asked me.

I nodded. "All the pages about us were at the very back. Like they were trying to hide them. And yesterday when I was reading what they'd written at the front of the book, it seemed like Brittany suddenly got nervous," I told them. "She said something like, 'Oh, don't read that. It's silly,' and then she took the book away from me."

At first I hadn't wanted to tell everyone else about the book, but now that we were all talking about it together, it was kind of a relief. I didn't feel so singled out. And it was better to know the truth of what they really thought of us. Even if it was painful.

We glanced over at the little group that was gathered around Jerry, laughing and teasing him. They didn't seem to notice that we were watching them.

"What did it say about me?" Ashlin asked me softly.

I didn't really like having to tell them all the mean stuff I'd read, but I knew it would drive them crazy not knowing. I knew what it felt like to have people gossiping about you. "Stuff about how you look like a boy," I said.

Ashlin tried to cover up her short haircut with her hands. "It was my mom's idea to cut all my hair off before camp! Not mine." She frowned at all of us. "I'm not getting it cut again for the next six months."

Then Natasha wanted to know what had been said about her, and Laurel-Ann asked me again to tell her what her page said.

Ashlin's eyes narrowed as she watched the little group hovering around Jerry. "Look at them over there. They're so two-faced."

Natasha pushed her glasses up on her nose. "I'm just so shocked. What do they have against us? We never did anything to them."

"It's Katherine," Laurel-Ann insisted. "It's her book, remember? She probably wrote all the comments."

I shook my head. "I don't think so. There was a list. Like each one of them had taken a turn and written a comment."

"Well, I'm sure it was Katherine's idea. She started it. I've been trying to tell you guys, I know her. I know how mean she can be when she really wants to be."

"Oh, no. I've actually seen it firsthand." And then I told them the mushroom story. "She did that after she saw how much I liked it. And you should've seen how pleased she was with herself. I'm just glad it wasn't a baby bird that had fallen out of its nest."

Ashlin let out a little snort. "For real! She probably would've squished it, too."

I had a sudden flash of Katherine and me sitting on the bench together, playing "Heart and Soul."

Okay, maybe she was nice that one time. And maybe I did feel sorry for her because of her home life. But that didn't give her the right to go around putting dead fish in people's beds or writing a bunch of awful things in books.

"We should do something to Katherine. Something embarrassing. Let's try to think of some way to embarrass her in front of Jerry," Laurel-Ann suggested. "We can't let her get away with this. She needs to learn that she can't go around saying mean things about people."

"Everybody ready?" asked Rachel. She had her backpack on and was trying to get Jerry's admirers to leave him alone. "Let's move 'em out!"

Katherine was about to put on her backpack when Brittany walked over to her. "Hey, do you have my book, by any chance? I never got it back last night."

"Oh yeah, I think I do have it," said Katherine, and then she unzipped her backpack and took out the pink book.

"Okay, great. And thanks for drawing all those funny pictures in it," said Brittany. "It'll be a great way for me to remember all the hikes we've been on."

The four of us gave each other quick looks. "Wait a second! I thought that was Katherine's book," Laurel-Ann whispered. "It's Brittany's?"

I shrugged. "I guess so. I just assumed it was Katherine's because she was always the one writing in it."

"Well, what does it matter whose it is?" murmured Ashlin. "It doesn't change the stuff they wrote about us."

"Girls, let's go!" Rachel called to us, because the others had already started walking away while we stood there whispering together. So we quickly put on our backpacks and caught up with the rest of them.

Ashlin was literally glaring at Brittany and the other girls as we walked along. "Are you okay?" asked Brittany. "You look upset about something."

"Oh, no. I'm fine. Couldn't be better," Ashlin answered her in a really snotty tone. Brittany gave her a surprised look and kept walking.

Ahead of us, we could see the ridges of the mountains against the horizon in different shades of purple. In front of them was a forest of thick green trees. But our group didn't seem to notice the beautiful landscape around us. Even though it was a sunny morning, I could almost picture dark storm clouds hovering over our heads.

It didn't take us that long to get back into camp. Ashlin and Natasha were walking with us toward the cabins. "I think you're right, Laurel-Ann," said Ashlin. "We should do something to get back at them. What can we do that'll be really embarrassing?"

"The first thing we've got to do is get that book

away from Brittany and tear all those pages out," said Laurel-Ann.

"You mean destroy the evidence? Then we won't have any way to prove they did it," said Natasha.

"Well, doesn't it bother you knowing that those mean things they said about us are out there? In writing?" Laurel-Ann's voice rose with emotion. "Other people could see them and read them too!"

"Yeah, that's true," agreed Ashlin. "I do want to rip all those pages out at some point, but I also want to do something to them. They've got it coming to them."

I didn't know what to think about this whole revenge thing. In some ways, I felt like they deserved it. Kind of like Boo deserved what Shelby had been doing to her. Those notes weren't really mean or anything, but they were just enough to make Boo wonder what was up. Plus, they'd seemed to cure her of her gossiping, at least for the time being.

But then it worried me a little too. I wasn't sure what Ashlin had in mind. And I didn't really want to get into some big war with Katherine and the other girls.

"Maybe we should just tell them that we saw what they wrote about us," I suggested. "All four of us, together. If we walked right up to them and repeated all the things they'd written about us, they'd be so embarrassed. I can just imagine the looks on their faces when they realize we've found out."

I could feel my heartbeat speed up at the thought of our group facing off with theirs. I'd never be able to do it alone, but with Laurel-Ann, Natasha, and Ashlin by my side, I'd be happy to.

I remembered how completely alone I'd felt at the beginning of camp when I'd first found out that people were talking about me. And even though I tried to ignore it, of course it bothered me. It was a huge relief now that I wasn't the only one being picked on.

"I don't know, Kayla. Do you really think that's a good idea?" asked Laurel-Ann. "They'll just deny it."

"We just have to plan some way to get back at them," said Ashlin. "There are four of us. If we work on this together, I know we'll come up with some kind of great revenge." She rubbed her hands together and grinned.

Hearing the way Ashlin said "revenge" made me a little nervous. But there was one thing I was glad about. At least were all in this together.

CHAPTER 17

Friday, July 4

"But there must be some things you're looking forward to about living in Florida," said Laurel-Ann.

"I guess so. We'll be close to the beach. And I've always been interested in marine biology. I would love to see dolphins, wouldn't you? Not in a water park, but out in the ocean."

Laurel-Ann sighed. "That would be amazing, wouldn't it? I bet there'll be all kinds of cool things you can do once you move there."

We were sitting up on Lakeview Rock, which was this massive rock formation at the end of the lake. This was the spot where we had all the campfires, because the top of the rock was big enough for everybody in camp to gather here and sit in a big circle.

But at the moment, Laurel-Ann and I had the rock to ourselves, and we were watching the swimmers below us. It was late in the afternoon, and we'd had a busy day of Fourth of July activities—a capture-the-flag game in the morning and then a campwide hide-and-seek, where all the campers tried to find the counselors, this afternoon.

"Oh, I almost forgot! When my parents first told us we were moving, my dad said that maybe the whole family could learn to scuba dive. But since they'd just made the big announcement about the move, I was too upset to even care about that. Of course, I didn't act upset. All along, I've acted like I'm just fine with the move."

I stretched out on my stomach and propped my chin on my hands. "But my mom can tell that it bothers me. She's tried talking to me about it. I just haven't felt like it. Till now."

"My mom's like that too. She always wants to fix everything, and sometimes the problems I have, she can't fix," said Laurel-Ann.

"I know exactly what you mean. Like this whole moving issue. If I tell her how upset I am about it, she'll just feel bad and think maybe she shouldn't have taken this job. I know the move is something our family needs to do, but that doesn't mean I'm going to be thrilled about it. I'm just trying to accept it, but it's not easy."

Laurel-Ann smiled at me. "Do you really think you'll learn to scuba dive? That would be so awesome!"

"I know! Wouldn't it? When my dad first mentioned it, I thought, 'Yeah, right. Scuba diving.' I thought he was just saying that. Almost like a bribe, you know? Like when you're a little kid and you have to get a shot, and you're screaming, but then they hand you a sucker. I never really cared about the stupid sucker! I didn't want to get poked in the arm in the first place!"

We were both laughing. Who knew that Laurel-Ann, who was such a talker, could also be a great listener? For days now, I'd been pouring my heart out to her, telling her about all the feelings I'd been having for months that I'd never wanted to talk about with anyone. Not even Danielle.

"How does Samantha feel about moving?" asked Laurel-Ann.

"Oh, she's excited about it. She thinks it'll be this great adventure. I used to be that way too when I was younger. It just seems like it's easier at that age. You change schools in second or third grade, and after two weeks, it feels like you've always been there." I sighed. "But now it's different. It gets harder to be the new girl."

"But Kayla, you're so much fun to be around. You're pretty, you're really talented. People just naturally like you. You'll do fine at your new school."

I smiled at her. It was nice to hear her saying all those things about me. "I hope so. I just don't want to come off as snobby and unfriendly. Now that I know some people have that impression of me, I'll always be worried about that. But if I try too hard to be the opposite of snobby, I'll come off as fake."

"No, you won't! I never thought that about you. I liked you from the first day."

That made me laugh. "I know! You have to admit, I wasn't that friendly to you. You tried so hard to be nice to me, though. Thanks for being so persistent."

I had a sudden feeling of déjà vu. Why did this seem so familiar? I tried to think of what it was, but the memory that had just come to me fluttered away, like a butterfly on a warm breeze.

"I'm just glad we're friends now," said Laurel-Ann.

"Yeah. Me too."

CHAPTER 18

Saturday, July 5

"Stop laughing!" I said to Laurel-Ann.

Laurel-Ann sucked in her cheeks. "I'm not laughing," she tried to say. But it's almost impossible to talk when you're sucking in your cheeks.

That did it. Now we were both about to lose control. "Don't laugh! Don't laugh!" I kept whispering to her. "He can't help it that he's rhythmically challenged!"

"Rhythmically challenged!" shrieked Laurel-Ann. She covered her mouth with both hands to keep from cracking up.

We were standing practically nose to nose in Pine Haven's crowded dining hall. All around us were dancing couples, and the music was so loud and pounding that it was making my eardrums vibrate. The Camp Crockett boys were here for our second dance, and amazingly, tonight my friends and I were dancing with actual boys.

Laurel-Ann and I were about to fall over because I'd just finished dancing with a boy who had the weirdest moves we'd ever seen. He reminded me of a puppet with strings attached to his arms and legs. While I was dancing with him and trying not to look at him, Laurel-Ann had stood off to the side, making funny faces at us. Every time I looked at her, I was terrified I was going to burst out laughing in the poor guy's face.

"Look at Shelby," I said. Since neither one of us could stop giggling, we needed some kind of distraction.

"I know! She's having such a great time," said Laurel-Ann.

Shelby had been dancing with the same boy all night. Laurel-Ann had danced with two different boys so far, and I'd danced with the puppet-on-a-string guy.

Since we were hot and thirsty, we moved over to the refreshment table and got some cookies and bug juice. I sipped my drink slowly and looked around.

"Can you believe how popular we are tonight?" I joked. "These Camp Crockett boys appreciate us now. We must have wowed them last time with our amazing moves."

"Wowed them? Wowed them?" Laurel-Ann went into hysterics over that remark.

"It's a real word!" I insisted. "I think the counselors are piping in laughing gas without telling us!"

Laurel-Ann nodded in agreement. "Mussage eight."

"What?" I shouted over the loud music. "What's does 'mussage eight' mean?"

When Laurel-Ann heard that, she spewed out bug juice everywhere. "I said . . . I said," but I couldn't understand her, because she could not stop laughing. She tried to catch her breath, but every time she looked at me, she cracked up again. "I said, 'My sides ache!'" she finally managed to say.

People were starting to stare at us, which made it even harder to get ourselves under control.

Natasha and Ashlin walked up and gave us surprised looks. "What's so funny?" asked Ashlin.

I shook my head. "It's hard to explain." I knew if I tried to tell her all the things that Laurel-Ann and I had been laughing about, she'd never get it.

"Well, we were just wondering—have you thought of any good ways to get back at Katherine and everybody?" she asked.

"Not really." Laurel-Ann had suggested that on the next hike, we should push Katherine into some poison ivy, but then we decided that it wouldn't be very embarrassing for her, just itchy.

"We haven't either," said Natasha.

"Well, guess what I found out today?" asked Ashlin. "The final campout is next week. So that would be the perfect time for us to put our plan into action."

Ashlin was wearing a skirt and a lacy blouse tonight, and she had on earrings and makeup, too. It seemed like the boy comment had bothered her as much as their mean remarks had bothered me.

"Katherine should be our main target," said Laurel-Ann. "I know she started it. I just know it. I still think she might be the only one who wrote all those things. I mean, we know someone did it, but we don't know they all did it. Maybe Brittany and Erin are completely innocent, and we don't want to go blaming——"

"Don't look now," I whispered suddenly to Laurel-Ann. "Someone's checking you out." A boy standing near us was looking in our direction. But he was mostly looking at Laurel-Ann.

She tried to see out of the corner of her eye. "Nobody's checking me out."

"Oh yes, he is!" said Natasha.

"It's because you look so gorgeous with your hair down," I told her.

Laurel-Ann's cheeks turned pink. "I do not!"

"Yes, you do. It really makes you look older," I said. "Walk across the floor like you're going to throw your cup away and see if he doesn't ask you to dance."

At first Laurel-Ann didn't want to move, but I gave her a little push. So she moved toward the trash can, and just as I had predicted, the boy walked over to her and they started talking. Laurel-Ann gave me a quick glance, and I could see the huge smile on her face.

Ashlin grinned. "You're such a matchmaker."

"I know. Want me to find someone for you?" I offered, looking around at the group of boys standing off to the side, watching all the dancers.

"No thanks. We need to find our counselor Jamie and help her with something," said Natasha.

"Yeah, help her talk to her boyfriend. I think they had a fight. But keep thinking about one thing. Do you know what that one thing is? Revenge!" Ashlin chuckled gleefully and rubbed her hands together. Natasha pulled her away by the arm, and they left to go find their counselor.

I was glad Laurel-Ann was dancing, but I missed having someone to laugh with. Should I ask a boy to dance? I could. It had been that kind of night. I couldn't believe how much fun we were having. The last dance had been fun too, but nothing compared to this one.

Laurel-Ann and her guy passed by right in front of me, and I was in the middle of making a funny face at her when Katherine Sperling suddenly appeared out of nowhere.

"Is that your new best friend?" she asked.

"Hi, Katherine," I said. I'd barely seen her all week, only at assemblies and stuff. Which hadn't exactly broken my heart.

"Well, is she?" she asked again.

"Yes, we're friends," I said.

Katherine was dressed the same way tonight as at the last dance—a plain T-shirt and jeans. And she still hadn't brushed her hair. For a minute I felt sorry for her. But then I remembered everything that had happened.

"How come you never practice anymore?" she asked. "I've looked for you in the lodge almost every day, and you're never in there."

Because a cat can play the piano better than I can, I felt like saying. Instead I just shrugged. "No reason."

"Kayla, are you mad at me about something?" asked Katherine in a soft voice. That almost got to me too. She had the same unhappy look in her eyes that she'd had when she was telling me about her family problems.

I could just tell her. Let her know that I'd read their

comments in the book, just to see what she would say. Would she admit to it? Or blame Erin and Brittany? Or act like she had no idea what I was talking about?

But if I did that, it would interfere with Ashlin's plans for revenge. They would know we were onto them.

"No, I'm not mad."

Katherine laughed. A rough laugh that sounded like sandpaper. "You got a funny way of showing it." She watched Laurel-Ann and the boy she was with. "It's because you're hanging out so much with her now, isn't it? What did she tell you about me?"

"Nothing," I said. I thought about letting Katherine know that Laurel-Ann had finally told me the Rainbow Trout story, but I kept quiet. I just wanted her to leave me alone.

Katherine was still staring at Laurel-Ann when she said, "Is she the one who's been telling people that when I was on a hike, I stepped on a baby bird?"

"What?" I practically shouted. "Laurel-Ann never said that!"

Katherine turned slowly to face me. "Did you?"

"No! I didn't say that either!" Although I had a sneaking suspicion who did.

Katherine looked over in Laurel-Ann's direction. "Just be careful who your friends are, Kayla. I used

to be friends with her too. Until she turned on me."
Katherine started to walk away, but then she stopped
and turned around. Her dark eyebrows came together
as she frowned at me.

"You never know when she might turn on you, too."

CHAPTER 19

Tuesday, July 8

"Is this going to be a really long hike?" asked Brittany as we piled into the van.

"Yep, really long," said Rachel. "You girls are the elite hikers—the finest of the fine. We know you can handle it."

"Really long?" Ashlin asked. "Like how many miles are we talking here?"

Jerry looked thoughtful. "Oh, ten. Twelve at the most."

"Are you serious? With backpacks? We'll never make it," Brittany moaned.

Lori was laughing, so I knew that Rachel and Jerry were teasing us.

"Can you at least tell us why we're supposed to wear swimsuits to go on a hike?" asked Erin. We all had our suits on under our clothes. They'd also told us to wear shoes we wouldn't mind getting wet.

Jerry was standing outside the van by the open driver's door. He looked up at the clear blue sky overhead and said, "In case it rains."

It was just after breakfast, and we were about to leave on the hiking honor trip. This trip was special. Unlike the other overnights and hikes we'd been going on all summer where anyone who wanted to go was welcome, the honor trips were by "invitation only."

Yesterday during assembly, Rachel had announced this trip and read off the names of the girls who had been asked to go: Brittany Choo, Natasha Cox, Erin Harmon, Laurel-Ann Humphreys, Ashlin Phelps, Katherine Sperling, and Kayla Tucker.

Afterward, Ashlin and Natasha had found Laurel-Ann and me in the crowd. They were both so excited because Ashlin had come up with a really simple plan to get back at Katherine's group. We were amazed at what a funny idea it was. And it was a great way to embarrass all three of them.

Laurel-Ann and I were on the very back bench.

Ashlin and Natasha were on the middle one, and Brittany, Erin, and Lori took seats on the front bench.

"Okay, looks like everybody's in," said Rachel. She was about to close the side door.

"Wait. What about Katherine?" asked Erin. "She's not here yet."

"Oh, Katherine's not coming," Rachel announced. She slid the door closed and climbed into the front passenger seat. Laurel-Ann and I exchanged quick looks.

"Not coming? How come?" asked Brittany. "She got invited."

Rachel looked over her shoulder at us. "I don't know. She told me before breakfast this morning that she was staying in camp. She wasn't feeling very well."

"Bummer! I can't believe she's missing the honor trip," said Erin.

I leaned forward to talk to Natasha and Ashlin in front of us. "Katherine's not coming?" I whispered. "That changes things a little."

"We won't be able to go through with our plan now," said Laurel-Ann. "We'll have to think of something else since Katherine's not here."

"No, we won't," said Ashlin. "It'll still work. We'll do it just like we planned. Katherine won't be there

177

tonight, but when she finds out later what happened, she'll still be really embarrassed."

"Whisper, whisper!" said Lori, turning around in her seat to look at us. "What's so secretive back there?"

"Nothing," said Laurel-Ann, so then we had to get quiet.

It was a luxury for us to be riding in a van with air-conditioning and a radio. But we hadn't been driving very long before we turned off the highway onto a winding road.

"Oh, I know where we're going!" Erin exclaimed.

Laurel-Ann looked out the window. "Oh, me too! I love this place!"

We'd pulled into a big parking area with lots of cars and people walking around.

"Is this where we're hiking?" asked Ashlin once Rachel had opened the doors and we were all climbing out.

"We thought we'd stop here first at Sliding Rock and do a little hiking later," said Rachel with a big smile.

Everyone started applauding and cheering. I wasn't sure what all the excitement was about.

"It's a good idea to keep your shorts on," Lori recommended. "Unless you want to rip a hole in your swimsuit." We left our T-shirts in the van and followed the crowds moving across the parking lot.

I soon found out why everyone was so happy to be here. It was a huge natural rock slide with water from a mountain stream rushing down. Off to one side, people were lined up behind handrails in the area where you climbed to the top of the big slab of rock.

We watched as swimmers took turns walking across the top of the rock and then sitting down where the water came rushing past. Then they'd slide all the way down to the bottom, feetfirst into a body of water at the base of the rock.

We walked up to the back of the line to wait our turn. It was really shady here, with trees all around us, and overlooking the rock was a wooden observation deck where people could watch if they didn't want to get wet.

"I bet that water is freezing!" Ashlin said to us.

"It is. Trust me," said Erin, in front of her in line.

"Trust you? You think we should trust you?" Ashlin asked her.

Erin looked surprised by Ashlin's reaction. She turned around and didn't say anything else.

Once we made it to the top of the rock, Erin and Brittany were the first ones to go down.

"I hope they both lose their swimsuits when they hit the bottom," said Ashlin.

 179

"Why are you so mad at them?" asked Laurel-Ann. "Katherine was the one who started it, and she's not even here right now."

"As far as I'm concerned, they're just as guilty as she is. They were all laughing on the first overnight, and Kayla said that it looked like more than one person had written something."

It was Ashlin and Natasha's turn to go now, so we watched them as they took their turn sliding down the rock into the water below.

"Ready?" asked Laurel-Ann. "It's scary at first, but I promise you'll love it."

The two of us walked carefully along the top ledge of the rock. We held hands because the wet rock was so slippery I was afraid we could topple over at any time. When we got to the spot on the rock where the water was rushing the fastest, Laurel-Ann sat down and showed me how I should sit behind her and hold on to her waist so we could go down together.

The water was icy, icy cold, a lot colder than the lake water at Pine Haven even, and I'd always thought that was the coldest water I'd ever felt in my life. Once we got going, we slid down so fast it gave me butterflies in my stomach, and then we both plunged into the body of water at the bottom.

When I came up for air, my lungs felt paralyzed from the cold. It took me a couple of seconds before I could catch my breath. "It's like ice water!" I yelled.

"I know! Don't you think it's refreshing?" Laurel-Ann laughed.

We swam over to the edge and climbed out, then got right back in line.

Our whole group had gotten separated in the line by now. Erin and Brittany were pretty far in front of us, and there were other people behind them. Rachel, Jerry, and Lori were together in another group.

But Ashlin and Natasha had waited for us. "This is so much fun!" said Ashlin, shaking off beads of water. "But do you know what's even more fun? Revenge!"

We were all laughing at the way Ashlin said that word.

"Are you sure this is still a good idea?" asked Laurel-Ann, giving each braid a twist to squeeze the water out. "I don't know if we should go through with it without Katherine. Can't we postpone this for now and think of something to do to her after we get back to camp?"

"No way!" said Ashlin. "We've got everything planned out perfectly. Tonight's the night!"

"I can't wait to get my hands on that book. I want to see for myself all those things they wrote about us," said

Natasha. Her arms were folded in front of her, and she was shivering a little.

Laurel-Ann's eyes widened. "Oh, no! I just thought of something! What if Brittany didn't bring her book this time? If we don't have the book, we can't go through with it."

Ashlin just smiled at her. "I already thought of that. I bought a blank notebook at the camp store and brought it along in case we need it as a backup. Pens, too."

"She thinks of everything," said Natasha.

"Look, it's our turn next," I said.

"Hey, let's form a chain—all four of us," Natasha suggested. So we all got into a line with Natasha in the very front and me in the back.

It was hard to say which was more fun—going down one at a time or as a group. Either way, it was such a rush to sit down and feel the water start to move you down the sloping face of the rock. The closer you got to the bottom, the faster you'd start to go. And every single time, it was a shock to hit that cold water down below. Then we'd run to get back in line for another turn.

We spent the whole morning at Sliding Rock, going down a dozen times. Sometimes we'd go down alone, sometimes in pairs, sometimes a bunch of us together. At one point, we got our whole group together for a huge chain, with Lori and Rachel in front and Jerry as the last link at the rear.

Then we stopped and ate our sack lunches at the picnic tables in the park after changing out of our wet clothes. When we all got back into the van after lunch, I felt like I was ready for a nap.

At least we were able to rest during the van ride. When we turned onto a gravel road and pulled the van over, we all dragged ourselves out and put on our backpacks.

"Are we seriously going on a really long hike now?" Laurel-Ann asked.

"Hey, is that any way for the best hikers from Pine Haven to talk?" asked Rachel.

We really couldn't complain, because it was true—our group had gone on the most hikes of any of the other Middlers. Everyone was pretty quiet as we started up a road with tall trees along both sides of it. "Is this a hiking trail?" asked Brittany.

"It'll take us where we're going," said Jerry.

We'd hardly gone far at all before we got to a clearing where we could see a log cabin at the top of a hill right in front of us.

"Uh, I think we might be on private property," said Natasha.

"It's okay." Jerry gave her a wink. "I know the owner."

We had all slowed down because we were obviously walking into someone's front yard. But Jerry didn't seem at all worried.

Then he walked right up onto the porch, pulled out a set of keys, and unlocked the front door. "Ladies, welcome to my home," he said, swinging the door open. "Please—try not to destroy it."

"Is this a joke?" gasped Erin. "This is your cabin?"

"Yep. We're staying here tonight," said Rachel with a laugh. "We just hiked up Jerry's driveway!"

"Well, what are you all waiting for?" he asked. "Go inside and have a look around!"

We all left our backpacks on the front porch and walked inside. There was a big open room with a stone fireplace, and a small kitchen at the back of the house. A narrow staircase led up to a loft above us. It had a real woodsy look to it, but it was also really cool.

"Oh my gosh! This is so adorable!" Brittany squealed. "You actually live here? "

Laurel-Ann nudged me. "Katherine is going to be so jealous when she finds out we got to spend the night in Jerry's cabin."

I smiled and nodded. I hadn't told Laurel-Ann about

the conversation I'd had with Katherine at the dance Saturday night. I knew it would just upset her. I had the feeling that Katherine didn't want to come on the honor trip because she'd been really hurt by the way I'd acted toward her.

It was strange to think that Katherine had been coming to Pine Haven for years, but she didn't seem to have any friends. I was probably one of the few people who'd been nice to her. I was starting to feel a little sorry for her, remembering the time we'd played the piano together. But then I reminded myself of that mean streak of hers.

"Okay, here's the sleeping arrangement," Jerry announced. "You girls can spread out sleeping bags down here in the living room wherever you can find a spot. And I'll be upstairs in my nice comfortable bed. Hope my snoring doesn't bother you."

"I get the couch!" said Rachel, rushing over to plop herself down on it.

"No, you take the loveseat and give me the couch," said Lori. "You're short enough to fit on it."

The two of them were arguing playfully about who should sleep where.

Ashlin gave us a devilish grin. "Can you believe how perfect this is? It's even better than if we were camping out. It'll make it that much easier for us to carry out our plan!"

"You love this, don't you?" I asked her. I couldn't keep from laughing.

Ashlin just smiled. "You know what they say. Revenge is sweet!"

CHAPTER 20

Jerry, Lori, and Rachel had gone outside and were lounging on the lawn furniture under some shade trees while we were all inside trying to pick our spots for tonight.

"Look, we can line up four sleeping bags in a row right here in front of the fireplace," Ashlin suggested.

"Hey, can we squeeze in here too?" asked Erin, coming through the front door with her sleeping bag. Brittany was right behind her.

"No, you can't," said Ashlin. "There's not enough room. You and Brittany can sleep back there." She pointed to the far corner of the living room, on the other side of the couch and loveseat.

Brittany dropped her sleeping bag at her feet.

"Okay, what's going on? You're all being really cold to Erin and me. What are you so mad about?"

Ashlin raked one hand through her hair. "You should know!"

Brittany and Erin both stood there with confused looks. "No, we don't know," said Brittany.

"Just forget it," Ashlin said. "Everything will be fine if you two stay over there in your spot and we'll stay in ours."

"Whatever," said Erin, shaking her head and walking away so she could spread out her sleeping bag.

"The backpacks are all out on the porch," Ashlin whispered to us. "As soon as we get our hands on the book, we can get started. Let's go."

We followed her out the door. Luckily, Brittany and Erin had stayed inside after that little exchange we'd had with them.

"Somebody guard the window in case they try to spy on us," said Ashlin.

I stood in front of the window, and Natasha pressed her back against the front door. "If they come barging through it, I might not be able to stop them. You know what a mouse I am."

"Shhh!" said Ashlin. She had crept over to where all the backpacks were lying in a jumbled pile. "Which one's Brittany's?" she hissed at us.

"I don't know. They all look the same," I murmured. We watched as Ashlin dropped to her knees and unzipped one backpack after another.

"What if she didn't bring it?" Laurel-Ann reminded us again.

"I told you. I've got that covered." Ashlin fumbled around through the backpack in front of her.

"This is making me so nervous!" said Laurel-Ann. "I just know they're going to catch us!"

"Here it is! I got it!" Ashlin whispered, pulling the pink book out of one of the backpacks. She looked around nervously. "How are we going to do this without anyone seeing what we're up to?"

"Stick it under your shirt," I advised. "Then we'll just walk away. Casually. Very, very casually."

So Ashlin tucked the book into the waistband of her shorts and pulled her shirt down. Then we all walked off the porch. Jerry, Rachel, and Lori waved to us as we strolled past them.

"We're just going to explore a little," said Ashlin.

"Have fun," they told us.

We walked across Jerry's backyard. When we were far enough away from the cabin and under the cover of some trees, Ashlin pulled the book out of her shirt. "Okay, let's just see what our friends had to say about us." She flipped to the pages in the back of the book and started reading. Natasha looked over her shoulder.

Laurel-Ann walked away from them. "I don't even want to see it. It'll upset me too much."

I had no desire to see what they'd written either. Once was enough for me.

Ashlin slammed the book shut. "Okay, now I definitely want to do this!"

"I think we should rip those pages out," Laurel-Ann suggested.

Ashlin nodded. "I think you're right. Because once we're finished making our little changes to the book, they're going to be really out of place in there."

"Can I have the honor?" Laurel-Ann asked, holding out her hand.

"Okay, go ahead." Ashlin handed her the book, and Laurel-Ann flipped to the back, then started ripping out the pages. She was about to tear them into shreds when Ashlin stopped her.

"Wait. Don't do that. Let's keep these as evidence. Things could get pretty ugly at some point, and we want to have proof of what they did to us." Ashlin took the pages from her and folded them up neatly before sticking them in her pocket.

"Okay. Let's get started." Ashlin sat down in the

grass, and we all took spots beside her. She pulled out the pen and opened Brittany's book to the very front. The first few pages were covered with the pictures Katherine had drawn of Jerry. She looked at us and smiled. "This is going to be so easy."

Inside the front cover, Ashlin wrote in large letters: "Jerry's Fan Club. President: Katherine Sperling. Vice President: Brittany Choo. Secretary: Erin Harmon."

On page after page of the drawings of Jerry, Ashlin wrote captions that were supposedly written by Katherine, Erin, and Brittany. Each one was about how great they thought Jerry was.

Then Ashlin ripped out the page where they had asked what they liked best about Pine Haven and the first overnight trip. She also tore out any pages of cartoons that didn't feature Jerry. "I don't think we need those. But we can definitely add a little here."

Ashlin added new pages asking more questions: "What do you like most about Jerry?" "Katherine: His smile." "Brittany: He has a great tan!" "Erin: His nice eyes."

"When did you first realize you had a crush on Jerry?" "Katherine: The first time I laid eyes on him." "Brittany: YES!! Definitely the moment I saw him." "Erin: Me too!"

I laughed when I saw what she'd just written. "How did you come up with all this?" I asked.

"Oh, I've been planning it all day," said Ashlin gleefully. She went on writing more questions and answers while the rest of us kept quiet and watched.

"Okay," Ashlin said finally. "I think that's pretty good. The whole book is dedicated to how wonderful Jerry is from his not-so-secret admirers." She passed it around for all of us to read.

"Now for the delivery," said Ashlin. She hid the book under her shirt again, and we all walked back toward the cabin.

"How are we going to do this?" I asked. "We can't all four go upstairs to Jerry's room and leave the book there. That will look really suspicious."

"I'm not going to do it!" said Laurel-Ann. "I know I'll get caught. I'll do something clumsy like knock over a lamp and break it and everyone will come running to see what's going on and—"

"Shhh!" warned Ashlin. "I'll do it. The rest of you act as lookouts."

Brittany and Erin were now sitting in the grass talking to Rachel, Jerry, and Lori when we walked past them. We went inside, and Ashlin asked us to stand guard while she tiptoed up the stairs and left the book on Jerry's bed.

I was starting to have second thoughts about this. Yes, they'd written mean comments about us, but they hadn't gone out of their way to embarrass us in front of everyone. And Laurel-Ann was probably right—Katherine likely was the one who'd started it all. But it was too late now. Ashlin was determined. So who was I to stop her?

Ashlin came tiptoeing back down the stairs with a big grin on her face. She gave us a thumbs-up. "Let's go back outside," she suggested.

We spent the rest of the afternoon exploring the woods around Jerry's cabin. Erin and Brittany stayed away from us, and we avoided them, too.

Laurel-Ann was really quiet, and I could tell she was upset about something. But with Ashlin and Natasha always around, it was hard for us to talk. I knew it bothered her that Katherine wasn't here. She would've loved to see Katherine embarrassed to death in front of Jerry. It would've made up for the whole Rainbow Trout incident.

For dinner, we were grilling hamburgers and hot dogs. The whole group was sitting around outside while Jerry lighted the grill.

"Hey, would one of you ladies go to the shed and get the new bag of charcoal in there?" he asked. "It's on the bottom shelf just inside the door."

"I'll do it," said Laurel-Ann, jumping up.

She motioned for me to follow her. As we walked across the yard together, she started whispering. "I have to tell you something. But you have to promise not to get mad at me."

"Okay, I promise."

We got to the shed and opened the door. Laurel-Ann had a completely panicked look on her face. "We have to get that book back. We have to! Erin and Brittany didn't write those things about us."

"You think Katherine did it by herself?" I asked.

Laurel-Ann grabbed one of her braids and twisted it so hard I was afraid she might pull her hair out. "No. It wasn't Katherine, either. I was the one who wrote them."

CHAPTER 21

"WHAT?"

"Don't get mad! You promised you wouldn't get mad!"

"What do you mean, you wrote them?" I screamed at her.

And then Laurel-Ann started crying and talking at the same time. The story rushed out so fast I felt like we were both flying out of control down Sliding Rock one last time.

"When I did it, I thought it was Katherine's book! I didn't know it was Brittany's! I never wanted to do anything to Brittany. Or Erin. It was just Katherine. Because we hate each other! And you were being nice to her. I wanted to be friends with you, but then

Katherine was trying to steal you away, and I knew she'd tell you all kinds of lies about me! And that's just the kind of mean thing she would do. I could just see her writing comments like that about all of us. I wanted to show everyone how mean Katherine really was. We were supposed to get back at Katherine!"

I stared at her with my mouth hanging open. "I can't believe this! Why didn't you stop us?"

"I tried!" she wailed. "I've been trying all day to talk Ashlin out of it. That's why I wanted to tear the pages out! I just wanted to take it all back and act like it had never happened!" Laurel-Ann was shaking with sobs.

Across the yard, we heard Jerry's booming voice. "Hey, where's my charcoal?"

I grabbed the bag off the shelf. "Stay here. I'll be right back." As I raced across the yard, I tried to think straight.

Now what? What were we going to do?

We could get the book back, but what would Ashlin and Natasha think when nothing happened? And what was I supposed to do with the book? Sneak it back into Brittany's backpack with all that stuff written in there? Or throw it on the grill and let it burst into flames?

I ran over and handed Jerry the charcoal, then walked slowly back to the shed where Laurel-Ann was waiting. As soon as she saw me she wailed, "You won't tell Ashlin and Natasha, will you? They'll hate me!"

I shook my head in frustration. "I don't know! Maybe we have to tell them now!"

"Kayla, please don't tell them! Please! I knew I could tell you because you're my friend. And a friend will stick by you, even in bad times. Right?"

I sighed. "Well, this is definitely a bad time!"

"Are you going to help me get the book back?" she asked in a tiny voice.

"Why don't you do it?" I snapped at her. "You got yourself into this. You can get yourself out!"

"I can't do it alone! I might get caught," she whimpered.

"I could get caught too!" I reminded her. "Or don't you care about that?"

Laurel-Ann covered her face with both hands and cried even harder. "I knew it! You hate me now!"

"Calm down," I told her. "I don't hate you. Stop crying and then go inside and wash your face. I have to think about what to do."

I left Laurel-Ann alone and went back to join the

others. Everyone was sitting around in lawn chairs, laughing and talking, while Jerry flipped burgers.

"Where's Laurel-Ann?" asked Natasha when I found a seat.

"Uh, she went inside to the bathroom," I said.

What if I told them right now? How would Natasha and Ashlin react? They'd be furious with Laurel-Ann. And they'd probably tell Erin and Brittany the whole story and show them the book. Then everyone would turn against her.

"All right. I've got hot dogs ready for whoever wants one. Paper plates are on the table," said Jerry.

Everyone else got up and headed for the picnic table, which was set up with napkins, buns, and plates, but I sank deeper into my lawn chair.

I had to help her, didn't I? She was my friend. And she'd been there for me when I was so upset about—

Wait a second. She'd comforted me when I was so upset about the comments that *she* had written! It was Laurel-Ann all along who'd said those things about me. Not Katherine. Not Brittany or Erin.

She wouldn't have written those comments if she didn't think there was some truth to them. Snobby rich girl? So unfriendly? Maybe that really was what she thought of me.

Suddenly I could see Katherine's face before me with that warning look. *You never know when she might turn on you, too.*

"Aren't you hungry?" asked Rachel, coming over to pat my shoulder.

"I guess so," I said, even though the last thing on my mind right now was food.

Laurel-Ann came out of the cabin, and since it was getting darker by the minute, no one seemed to notice that she'd been crying. Since everyone was around now, there was no way we could talk. All she could do was give me a worried look as we filled our plates.

I was quiet as I took my plate back to my lawn chair and sat down, but my mind was racing. I watched Laurel-Ann nibbling silently on her hot dog. We only had a few hours before we'd all go to bed. And then Jerry would find the book.

How would he react? He'd just laugh about it. Maybe he wouldn't even say anything about it because he wouldn't want to embarrass them. So it might be okay.

But then maybe not. Maybe he'd come down the stairs laughing and waving the book around. "Hey, I've got my own fan club!"

As soon as Brittany saw it, she'd recognize it. And then the whole story would come out.

My face felt hot when I thought about how we'd taken an innocent little book with a bunch of funny drawings in it and destroyed it. I tried to take a bite of hamburger, but I honestly felt like I was going to gag.

Natasha and Ashlin scooted their lawn chairs closer to mine. "Hey, what's up? You're being so quiet tonight," said Ashlin.

"I'm just tired. All that sliding wore me out," I said.

"Want some watermelon?" asked Natasha.

"No thanks. I'm stuffed." So they got up to get some slices for themselves.

What if when they came back, I told them I was having second thoughts? I really had wondered if we should go through with it, even before Laurel-Ann made that unbelievable confession.

She was still sitting there all by herself, picking at her food. I knew how miserable she was right now.

I knew how miserable I'd been and how much it had helped to have someone there to comfort me. But did it count when your friend was comforting you about a pain that she had caused?

But that wasn't the only time she'd been a good friend to me. She'd been there for me when I needed to talk to someone about the move. For the first time all summer, I was actually starting to feel better about moving. Thanks to Laurel-Ann.

Jerry had turned on a lantern and put it on the picnic table, and now Lori was organizing a watermelon-seed-spitting contest. She'd lined the others up, and they were all laughing and shouting as they took turns to see who could spit seeds the farthest. Neither Laurel-Ann nor I had moved from our chairs.

"Hey, has anyone seen my book?" asked Brittany. She'd just come back from the cabin. "It was in my backpack, but now I can't seem to find it."

I noticed Laurel-Ann's expression. She looked like her dog had just died. Everyone was asking Brittany about the book. What did it look like? When had she seen it last?

"I wanted everyone to sign it," said Brittany. "So I'll have something to remember you all by."

Ashlin walked over to my chair. "Oh, that's okay," she whispered as she bent over me. "We signed it already." Then she spit a seed across the lawn and almost hit Jerry in the back of the leg.

"You can look for it in the morning," said Rachel. "It's hard to find anything in the dark."

Brittany sat down in a lawn chair, but from the

worried look on her face I could tell she was bothered that her book was missing.

There was no easy way out of this, was there? Anything I did or didn't do would cause a problem. But why was it even my responsibility?

I didn't write those nasty comments about the four of us. I didn't create the Jerry's Fan Club book. And I didn't leave it on his bed.

Maybe the best thing for me to do was to just stay out of it. Let whatever was going to happen, happen. If Laurel-Ann wanted the book back, she could get it herself.

Now everyone was throwing away their trash and watermelon rinds and cleaning up all the dinner things.

Rachel started singing a Pine Haven song. The last thing I felt like doing right now was singing. Everyone else joined in with a lot of energy, but I just mumbled the words.

And then after we'd sung about three or four songs, Rachel said, "Okay, now let's sing my favorite song. In three parts. Make new friends, but keep the old—"

"No, no, stop!" shouted Lori. "Why do you always want to sing rounds? That's not even really a song!"

"I know, right?" said Ashlin. "Why do you like to sing that all the time?"

Rachel just smiled at us. "Because it's short and sweet. And yet so profound."

Jerry laughed out loud when he heard that. "Yeah, just like you, Hoffstedder!"

Everyone burst out laughing over that comment, and then Rachel started singing again. She made us do it in three parts, with everyone coming in at different times.

"Make new friends, but keep the old—one is silver and the other gold. Make new friends, but keep the old—one is silver and the other gold. Make new friends, but keep the old—one is silver and the other gold."

Make new friends? It was my new friends who'd gotten me into this mess in the first place. It had been a mistake for me to ever get friendly with any of these girls. It had only led to trouble. I would've been better off just keeping to myself and going to activities alone. And they could sing all they wanted about keeping old friends, but I could tell them from experience: It wasn't all that easy.

I was really starting to hate that song.

Laurel-Ann had quietly pulled her lawn chair right next to mine. When I looked at her, she mouthed the words, "I'm sorry."

I just looked away.

We sat there in silence for a few minutes, and then Laurel-Ann stood up. I could see that tears were running down her cheeks. She walked away from our little circle of chairs and headed toward the cabin.

"Hey, where are you going?" asked Rachel.

"Bathroom," she said over her shoulder.

I waited for a few seconds and stood up. "I need to go too."

As I walked away I heard Jerry comment, "You ladies always go in pairs."

I followed Laurel-Ann inside, and as soon as the door was closed behind us, she completely lost it. "You hate me now!" she sobbed. "You really hate me!" Tears were streaming down her cheeks and she could hardly catch her breath, she was crying so hard.

"Laurel-Ann, I don't hate you. But yeah, I'm upset about this! I can't believe you did that! And blamed it all on Katherine." I let out a deep sigh. "And you know what else really bothers me? Maybe you really think those mean things you wrote about me. Is that how you really feel about me?"

Laurel-Ann shook her head so hard her braids were bouncing. But no sound was coming out of her mouth. I had to wait for her to stop crying enough so that she could say something. I remembered how she'd patted my back when I was crying. She could probably use a hug right now. But that was the last thing I felt like giving her.

"Don't you remember those things about me in that book? About how I never shut up and I'm such a loser who has no friends? That's what I really think about myself! I know people don't like me. I know I talk too much. I get nervous and I can't seem to stop myself. You're the first good friend I've ever had at Pine Haven." She burst out crying again. "I consider you my best friend. All summer, I've wanted to be friends with you. And then it finally happened. But now I've lost you, too!"

I stood there with my arms crossed. "You haven't lost me. I'm standing right here in front of you. Look, let's go get that book, right now. You and me."

I headed up the narrow staircase, taking the steps two at a time. Laurel-Ann was still standing by the front door, looking unsure about what to do. "Stay there and keep an eye out," I hissed.

My heart raced as I tiptoed into Jerry's room, feeling like a cat burglar. I grabbed the book, stuffed it in my shirt, and dashed out of there so fast I almost crashed into the wall as I rounded the corner. Then I bounded down the steps.

I stood panting in front of Laurel-Ann. "What are we going to do with it now?" I asked.

She shook her head. "I don't know! Should we put it back in Brittany's backpack?"

"No. She's looking for it. And she'll see all that stuff we wrote in there."

Laurel-Ann bit her lip. "Maybe we should just get rid of it. Throw it away in the woods or something."

I was starting to feel panicked. Any second now, someone could walk in and find us. "Here—you take it." I pulled the book out of my shirt and shoved it into her hands. "Hide it in your backpack. I don't want anything to do with it. You could put it in there on our way out," I said.

And then I walked out the door.

Whether I liked it or not, Laurel-Ann and I were now in this together.

CHAPTER 22

Wednesday, July 9

At least the rest of the night was uneventful. Brittany and Erin still couldn't figure out why we were shunning them, but they stayed in their own little corner of the living room and we stayed in ours.

The next morning Jerry came downstairs and announced we were having pancakes for breakfast. Then he organized everybody to help out, but he didn't mention one word about the book.

"What happened?" asked Ashlin. "I expected at least some remark about his fan club."

"I'm sure he saw it," said Natasha. "You left it right on his bed, didn't you?"

"Yeah. There's no way he could've missed it."

"I bet he'll give it back to Brittany privately," I suggested. "He knows she's looking for it. He probably doesn't want to embarrass her in front of everyone."

I hated this. I'd found out earlier this summer that I wasn't a particularly good liar, and that I'd eventually get caught. Already I was starting to get nervous.

After breakfast, we got busy rolling up our sleeping bags and getting things organized. Brittany came in from the porch with her backpack and dumped all the contents out on the floor. But there was no sign of her book. "Okay, where's my book? I still can't find it."

"Hey, everyone," shouted Ashlin. "Let's help Brittany find her book. Has anyone seen it? It's pink with yellow flowers on it."

I could see how Ashlin was watching Jerry for some reaction, but he didn't blink an eye. She was obviously frustrated that the fan club book wasn't making an appearance.

Rachel came out of the kitchen, wiping her hands on a dish towel. "Are you sure you brought it with you? Maybe you left it back at camp."

Brittany was on her knees, sorting through her clothes. "I'm sure I packed it. I made a point of bringing it, because I wanted everyone to write something in there."

"Well, maybe you meant to bring it, but it never made it into your backpack. Happens all the time. I bet you'll find it when we get back," Rachel assured her.

Ashlin walked right up to Jerry. "Have you seen a pink book with yellow flowers on it anywhere?"

He just shrugged his shoulders. "Can't say I have."

"Brittany's book has got to be here somewhere!" said Ashlin.

Laurel-Ann's face was deathly pale. "What if they want to search all our backpacks?" she whispered to me.

I shook my head. "I doubt it. Just stay calm."

Eventually Brittany gave up trying to find it. "I hope it's back in my cabin." She looked up at Ashlin. "Thanks for trying to help me."

We had a lazy morning just hanging around the cabin, and nobody else mentioned the book. Then in the afternoon, Jerry took us out bushwhacking. It was a tough hike through the woods without any kind of trail. A lot of it was downhill, too. We were slipping and sliding through a thick layer of dead leaves, grabbing onto tree trunks and branches to brace ourselves so we wouldn't go crashing down the mountainside.

My arms got all scraped up by twigs that swatted me as I slid past them, and I had streaks of mud down both of my legs. It was the hardest hike we'd ever done—a lot different from walking along an already cleared trail. We had to pay attention to how we were going to get through the underbrush and figure out the easiest path to take as we maneuvered through all the trees. The one good thing was that we weren't wearing our backpacks.

It was hot and exhausting and scary at times. But it was also the best hike I'd ever been on.

When we stopped to take a break, Rachel pointed to a tree with smooth gray bark. "Hey, everyone. Know what kind of tree this is? It's a beechnut. I'll show you something."

We watched as she went over and broke off a few twigs, then peeled off the bark. She put a little strip of it in her mouth and started chewing it.

"Are you eating that?" asked Brittany in amazement.

"No, just chewing it. It's got a minty flavor. Anybody else want to try it?" She handed us all a little piece and we popped it into our mouths. It did taste a little minty, but after a while it lost its flavor, so I spat mine out.

Jerry led us on a roundabout way back to his cabin. He kept giving us tips about what to do if we were ever lost in the woods.

"Look up, and try to see if there's a spot where there

aren't any trees. That will take you to some kind of clearing. Then you can look at where the sun is in the sky and try to figure out your direction."

"What if it's a cloudy day?" asked Brittany.

Jerry laughed. "That could be a problem."

Late in the day, we loaded up the van and got ready to leave. Brittany made one last search for her book, but since she didn't look in Laurel-Ann's backpack, of course she didn't find it. Then we all climbed into the van for the drive back to Pine Haven.

"I have an idea about what might have happened," said Ashlin, turning around in her seat to talk to Laurel-Ann and me. "Maybe he didn't turn the lights on when he went to bed last night, and the book fell on the floor. Maybe he never even saw it. Which means he still might find it later."

"How can anyone go to bed without turning on a light?" asked Natasha.

"I think he found it, but he's just keeping quiet about it so he won't embarrass them," I said.

"Well then, it didn't work! I'm so bummed that it didn't work!" said Ashlin. Laurel-Ann just stared out the window without saying a word.

The van pulled into Pine Haven about an hour before dinner. All I wanted to do was take a hot shower and then go see Samantha, but Shelby had lots of updates to give us when we got back to the cabin.

"Chris isn't mad anymore about the prank that got played on her before you guys left, so at least that drama is over," she told us.

I collapsed onto my bunk. "Great. Because the last thing I need right now is drama," I moaned.

"Why? Was there drama on the hiking trip?"

Laurel-Ann must have been practicing for a career as a mime, because she had not said one word.

"It's complicated," I said with a sigh.

"Oh, one other thing. Wayward and Gloria keep saying we have to enter an act for the talent show. I'm doing one with my Guard Start class, but all of those girls are in Cabin Two. So we need one for Cabin Four. I didn't exactly volunteer you, but I did mention what a great piano player you were." Shelby smiled sweetly at me.

"Wonderful. Any other bad news?" I asked.

"You don't have to play the piano. I just didn't think you'd mind," said Shelby.

"I don't mind, really. But I haven't practiced in a while." And suddenly I remembered Katherine. There was a lot I needed to talk to her about. And the sooner the better.

CHAPTER 23

As soon as I'd taken a hot shower, I went looking for Katherine. When I knocked on the door of Cabin 2, she was the only one inside. She came to the screen door, but she didn't open it.

"What do you want?" she asked cautiously.

"I wanted to talk to you," I said. "I'm sorry you didn't come on the honor trip with us."

"Did you have a good time with your new best friend?"

"We all had fun. But we also missed you."

"Yeah, right."

I wished she'd at least ask me to come in or come outside herself so that we didn't have to talk through this screen door.

"I know I wasn't really friendly to you the last time I saw you. And I'm sorry about that."

"So what happened? Did Rainbow Trout turn on you, and now you want to be my best friend?" Her tone was very sarcastic, but I could tell that her feelings were still hurt, and this was her way of covering it up.

"No. She didn't turn on me." There was no way I could tell her about any of the things that Laurel-Ann had done. I knew that was just the kind of stuff she wanted to hear. It would give her more reasons to hate her archenemy.

"It looks like I'm going to play piano for the talent show tomorrow. But I need to practice. Want to come to the lodge with me?"

That was enough to get Katherine to open the screen door. We walked to the lodge without talking, but when we got inside, I was starting to form a plan. "I thought maybe I could practice some, but I can also teach you a few more songs."

Katherine stood beside the piano bench and frowned. "Why are you suddenly being nice to me again?"

I sighed. "Look, I know I didn't treat you very well. I'm sorry. I'm trying to make it up to you. Is it so hard to believe that I want to be your friend?"

Katherine's eyes narrowed. "Yeah, it is. When you're used to friends treating you like dirt. How do I know you and Rainbow Trout aren't up to something together?"

I sat down on the piano bench and starting playing the C scale I'd taught her. "I guess you'll just have to trust me."

"Why should I?"

"I don't know, Katherine! I can't force myself on you. You can stay in here while I practice if you want. I'll show you something new if you want. If you don't want to, I guess you can leave."

I started playing the left-hand part to "Heart and Soul." She didn't come in with the right-hand part, because she was still standing there with her arms crossed. But I kept playing it. It sounded incomplete without the melody, and I hoped that would make her want to join me.

It took awhile, but finally she stuck her index finger out and hit middle C four times. She played the rest of the part standing behind me.

"That's good. You remembered it all."

"I've been practicing," she said softly. "Just because you haven't been coming in here doesn't mean I can't."

"Really?" I asked. "That's great! Want to switch places and play the left-hand part?"

Katherine shrugged, but when I scooted over on the bench, she took a seat and started playing. And she was playing three-fingered chords now.

"That's amazing! You really have been practicing!" I said as I came in on the right-hand part.

Katherine's mouth twitched into a smile. "I told you."

"It sounds great. I'll teach you something new, but first I was wondering about something. You never did tell me the Rainbow Trout story," I reminded her.

I figured it was time for me to hear Katherine's version of the story. "I know it was something that happened last summer. . . ."

Katherine nodded. "Yeah. We were friends last summer. Good friends. I told her a lot of secrets. About my family." She looked at me. "The same stuff I told you. Only I told her I didn't want her to tell anyone else. Those aren't the kinds of stories you want everyone in camp to hear, you know?"

"I didn't tell anyone about what you told me," I said.

"I knew you wouldn't. I could tell you were the kind of person who wouldn't go around talking about people. But Laurel-Ann isn't. She loves to gossip, in case you haven't noticed."

I felt absolutely frozen in place as I listened to Katherine.

Loves to gossip. Loves to gossip. In case you haven't noticed.

"So anyway, before I know it, everyone in the cabin has found out about my tragic life story. I asked Laurel-Ann if she'd told everyone, but she wouldn't admit to it. But then some of the other people in our cabin said that Laurel-Ann had been the one who told them. One day we were all mad at her and accusing her of what she did, and Megan Fitzpatrick said, 'Laurel-Ann, you've got a mouth on you as big as a rainbow trout.' And that's why I still call her by that nickname."

I was staring straight ahead at the keyboard. "Are there any fish in Pine Haven's lake?" I said suddenly.

"What?" asked Katherine.

"There aren't, are there? I've never seen any. Only tadpoles." I gazed at the white and black keys in front of me as if I was in a trance.

"What does that have to do with anything?" she asked.

I shook my head. "Nothing. It has nothing to do with anything."

Everything came rushing back to me. All those questions that Boo was always asking me when camp first started, Laurel-Ann was always there. She was there when we were talking about my mom's photograph,

217

there when I made the phone call and got the postcards, there when we were talking about why Shelby cried so much.

Boo was the one asking questions. But Laurel-Ann was the one taking notes.

I'd finally figured out who was responsible for all those rumors being spread around. And I was wrong. It wasn't Bubonic Boo.

It was Laurel-Ann. My new best friend.

CHAPTER 24

Thursday, July 10

I sat on my bottom bunk with my note cards in my lap. My hand was actually starting to cramp a little from all the writing I'd been doing, so I stopped to lay down the pen and wiggle my fingers. Scattered in front of me on the bed were all the letters and postcards I'd gotten from my friends this summer.

Even though everyone was supposed to be at activities, I was cabin-sitting, because I had something more important to do.

I don't know why, but I'd suddenly been inspired this afternoon to do something I hadn't done all summer— write letters.

I'd already finished Danielle's letter and Maricela's, and now I was on Emily's. I was telling them all how sorry I was that I hadn't written them. The one line I kept writing over and over was this one: Even though I haven't been good about keeping in touch so far, I promise I'll do better from now on.

When the screen door opened, I wasn't all that surprised to see Laurel-Ann.

"Hi. Do you mind if I come in here?" she asked.

"Of course not. It's your cabin too," I said.

I hadn't completely shunned her, but things really weren't okay between us. It was hard for me to even look at her, knowing all the problems she'd caused me this summer.

Laurel-Ann sat down on the edge of her bed. "You're writing letters. That's a good thing, right?"

I nodded and kept writing. Last week I'd told Laurel-Ann all about how I couldn't even make myself write to all my friends because I was still so sad about the move. She'd definitely helped me by listening to me talk about everything.

That made it even harder to deal with all this now. She'd been such a good friend to me in lots of ways. But at the same time such an awful one.

"You're still mad at me, aren't you? I really am

sorry, Kayla. And I never did thank you for helping me get the book back."

"You're welcome," I said. Last night I'd watched her stuff Brittany's book in the bottom of her trunk. I wondered what she planned to do with it, but it wasn't really my problem.

There was a long silence while I kept writing and Laurel-Ann watched me. The only sound was my pen scratching on the paper.

Finally she cleared her throat. "Do you think we'll ever be friends again?"

I folded up the letter I'd just finished and stuck it inside an envelope. "I don't know. I'm pretty mad about all this."

"But at least it's over now. We got the book back."

"This isn't just about the book!" I said suddenly. "There's a lot more to it than that!"

Laurel-Ann drew back with a stunned look on her face. "Why are you so mad at me?"

"Don't you know? Don't you know all the things you did to me? And not just me. You did them to Boo and Shelby, too. And Katherine, Brittany, and Erin! And let's see—who did I leave out? Oh, yeah. Natasha and Ashlin."

I was raking all the letters and postcards up off my

bed and trying to put them into a neat pile, but my hands were actually starting to shake. "And those are just the ones I know about! For all I know, the list could go on!"

"What are you talking about? What did I ever do to Shelby or Boo?" she asked. The whiny sound of her voice made me so mad I felt like walking over there and yanking on one of her braids.

"Laurel-Ann, I found out! I figured out that you were the one who was spreading all those rumors around. You were the one who was going around telling everyone that I was the daughter of a rich movie star. And you told everyone that Shelby's mother was dead. And you let us think that it was Boo! Shelby's been mad at her all summer because of that, and I blamed her too. And all the time, it was you!"

I was shocked by how mad I was getting. I was breathing hard and fast, and I could feel the blood pumping through all my veins. I watched Laurel-Ann's bottom lip start to quiver. All the tears in the world couldn't wash away what she'd done.

"I didn't . . ."

"Don't deny it! I know it was you! That just makes it worse for you to sit there and say you didn't do all those things. I know you did!"

Laurel-Ann couldn't hold back any longer. She burst into tears, and all I did was watch her. She covered her face with her hands and sobbed so loud I was afraid people outside would come rushing to see what was happening in here.

When she was finally able to take a breath, she looked up at me with red, puffy eyes.

"You're right! I'm a horrible person! I hate myself."

That made me so frustrated, I actually growled at her through clenched teeth. "Stop it! That doesn't help the situation. So you admit that you're the one who's been going around spreading all these rumors?"

She nodded. Seeing that she was at least willing to admit to it made me sigh with relief. "Why, Laurel-Ann? Why do you do it?"

Laurel-Ann shook with sobs. "I don't know why," she wailed. "I guess . . . I guess maybe I'm afraid that people are gossiping about me. So maybe that's why I do it first."

She wiped her tears away with the backs of her hands. She was sniffling so loudly that I got up and took some Kleenex off the shelf by Gloria's bed. I handed them to her without saying anything.

"The thing is, when I'm telling people some big secret about someone else, they're always really interested in me. They like hearing about other people, and so they listen to what I say." She blew her nose in the Kleenex several times and then sat there, shuddering.

"Well, yeah, they like hearing gossip about other people. But they hate hearing it about themselves! Don't you care about the feelings of the people you're talking about? Doesn't it bother you to know that you're telling some private thing about them that they don't want anyone else to know? Or even worse, that you're telling stuff about people that isn't even true?"

She sniffled a few times and stared at a spot on the floor. "I guess I'm not even thinking about that when I'm talking about them."

"You got that right!" I yelled. "You're not thinking! It's horrible what you're doing, Laurel-Ann. You've got to stop it! You'll never have any friends if you keep talking about them behind their backs."

"I don't have any friends now," she said sadly, shaking her head and staring at the floor. "I used to, but I've lost the only friend I ever had."

I grabbed my pillow and put up it to my face. Then I screamed into it as loud as I could. When I pulled it away, I glared at her. "Stop it! Stop being so dramatic. This isn't making it any easier. Yes, we were friends . . . are friends. You really can be a good friend at times. We had so much fun together, and I was able to talk to you about things. You were there for me when I needed you. But you've got to stop all this gossiping. Look at how many problems it's caused. And it almost cost you my friendship!"

I breathed deeply in and out. Sometimes a good scream will do you good.

She looked up at me with her red, tearful eyes. "Did it? Did it cost me your friendship?"

I shook my head. "I don't know. I'm still mad about this. It's not the kind of thing I can get over right away."

"But I'm really, really, really, really sorry, Kayla. I want you to forgive me."

"It's not just about me forgiving you. This is like . . . the biggest mess I've ever seen. Natasha and Ashlin don't like Katherine, Erin, or Brittany now. Katherine doesn't like you. Shelby doesn't like Boo, and you know what? It all comes back to you. It's like this big, tangled web that everybody's trapped in, and you're the big fat spider that spun it all."

I stopped talking and let all that sink in. That actually sounded pretty good. I was impressed with myself for thinking it up.

"But what do I do?" asked Laurel-Ann. "I can't tell them I'm sorry! They'll hate me!"

"Oh, you're right. So let's just let them all go on hating each other, even though they're not the ones who caused all this!" I snapped at her.

"Well, what am I supposed to do? I can't take it back. I wish I could, but I can't. How am I supposed to fix all this?" she whimpered.

I shook my head. "I have no idea. It's the biggest mess I've ever seen."

Laurel-Ann looked at me as if she'd just thought of something. "My mom's always telling me to make a list. She thinks if you write stuff down you can figure it out better. Maybe we should make a list."

"What kind of list?" I asked.

"I'm not sure. But maybe we should try it."

"Fine," I said. I grabbed a notepad from my shelf and tossed it to her. "Make a list."

CHAPTER 25

Friday, July 11

Laurel-Ann paced back and forth across the wooden floor of the lodge. "I'm so nervous. What if . . . what if she hits me or something?"

"She's not going to hit you," I assured her.

"She might. You don't know her the way I do."

"Actually, I think I do know her pretty well by now," I said.

I sat at the piano and practiced a scale series, anything to break the tension in the room right now. This was our last item on the list, and I figured it was probably going to be the hardest.

We'd had lots of things to do in the past two days. Laurel-Ann had first gone to Shelby and admitted that she was the one who'd told lots of people about her mom. Although I did feel a little guilty too. If I'd been better about keeping my own mouth shut, none of that would've happened.

Then we'd talked about what to do about Boo. We eventually decided to leave her one last anonymous note. *Dear Boo, Sorry for calling you Bubonic and leaving you these strange notes. Just a case of mistaken identity. Sorry about that.*

And now Katherine. I'd told her to meet me in the lodge so I could get the notebook back from her. That was another item on the list that we'd be able to check off. I'd given Katherine a blank notebook and asked her to recreate the funny drawings she'd done in Brittany's book. As far as she knew, Brittany's book had gotten lost on the honor trip, so we were making a new one for her.

Yesterday, Laurel-Ann and I had found Ashlin and Natasha. Laurel-Ann had explained to them everything that really happened with Brittany's book, and even though they were pretty mad about it, they'd taken it fairly well. And they'd signed the new book we were planning to give to Brittany.

Now we just had to get the new book from Katherine with her pictures in it. And Laurel-Ann was going to apologize to Katherine for what happened last summer.

I turned around when I heard footsteps.

Katherine had just walked in, but when she saw Laurel-Ann with me, she stopped dead in her tracks.

"Hi," said Laurel-Ann in a tiny voice.

Katherine looked first at Laurel-Ann, then at me. "Here's the book." She had a cautious look, as if she expected both of us to tackle her.

I got up from the bench. "Okay, great. She's really going to love getting this. Thanks for taking the time to draw those pictures again. We all loved your artwork."

"No problem."

Katherine and Laurel-Ann were just standing there, looking each other up and down. Not only did they hate each other, but I could tell there was some jealousy between them over me, also.

Last night for the talent show, I'd asked Katherine to be onstage with me to hold the sheet music and turn the pages at the right times. I didn't really have to have someone do that, but it helped. Sheet music had a way of not staying open, and it could get really annoying during a performance. I'd played Chopin's Prelude in E Minor, and Katherine had been thrilled to help me out. But I could tell it bothered Laurel-Ann.

"Laurel-Ann wants to tell you something," I said.

"Okay," said Katherine. She still had that look of distrust in her eye.

Laurel-Ann took a deep breath. "I'm sorry that I talked about you last summer. I know you told me all that stuff in private and I wasn't supposed to tell anyone. I'm sorry I did it."

Katherine shrugged. "All right. Whatever."

"And she wants to ask you something," I prompted.

Laurel-Ann gave me a quick glance and then looked at Katherine. "Would you please stop calling me Rainbow Trout?"

"Fine. I'll stop calling you Rainbow Trout."

Well, it wasn't the warmest apology I'd ever seen, but at least it was over. "And there's something I want to say. Tonight at the Circle Fire, I want to sit next to both of you."

We were having the final campfire tonight, and everyone had been talking all day about what a big deal it was. It was going to be really solemn, with people giving speeches and talking about what Pine Haven meant to them. And we'd be singing lots of camp songs, and then lighting candles at the end. Everyone said that it was really special, but also really sad because we were all going home tomorrow.

"This will be my first Circle Fire, and everyone says you should sit with your best friends. And I consider you both the best friends I have here."

"Well, okay, but I'm not friends with her. She can apologize, but I still don't want to be friends with her," said Katherine.

"I'm not asking you to start being friends," I said. "I just want you to stop being enemies. I want to be able to sit with both of you and not have you tossing dead fish at each other."

Laurel-Ann giggled at that, and even Katherine cracked a bit of a smile.

"So is it a deal?" I asked. "I'll sit in the middle between you two to make sure things don't get out of hand."

Katherine actually gave me a big smile over that. "It's a deal."

"It's a deal," agreed Laurel-Ann.

"Good," I said. "Let's take this notebook to Brittany."

"She's going to love it," said Laurel-Ann. She gave Katherine a quick look. "You really are a good artist."

"Thanks."

And so the three of us left the lodge together. I

couldn't believe it, but Laurel-Ann had done a pretty good job of untangling her web. There were still some sticky parts, and things weren't exactly perfect, but at least they were a lot better.

And I couldn't ask for much more than that.

CHAPTER 26

Saturday, July 12

"But what if I don't see them again? What if we don't come back? Gracie is my best friend, and Mary Claire's my other best friend. And I might never see them again." Samantha leaned against me in the van and sobbed.

We were on our way to the airport. It had been a really tearful scene when we'd left Pine Haven. Laurel-Ann couldn't stop crying, and so of course I'd cried too. And then as I was saying good-bye to Katherine, even she got really emotional. Katherine, who never let her guard down, hugged me tight and got all choked up when she tried to thank me for the piano lessons.

I'd told her that maybe she could get a keyboard to practice on, and even though private lessons could be expensive, sometimes you could take a group class. Or maybe there was a music program at her school. And there were online tutorials. She'd loved all those ideas.

And it was sad to say good-bye to Shelby, and even Boo, and all the Side A girls. I didn't really realize how much I was going to miss everyone until we were all saying good-bye.

"I don't know. We might come back next year. We can tell Mama and Daddy how much we liked it. So maybe we will come back," I told Samantha.

"I don't want to move to Florida! I want to go back to Maryland!" Samantha said suddenly. "Florida stinks!"

Reb Callison was sitting on the bench in front of us. When she heard that, she looked over her shoulder, and I could see her chuckling about that. "Florida doesn't stink! Well, maybe some parts of it smell a little fishy."

Now Samantha was giggling a little.

"It's going to be great. We'll be close to the beach, and it'll be warm and sunny. People come from all over the world to vacation in Florida, and we're going to be living there," I said. It was the same line Daddy had given me a few months ago, but it seemed like a good one to use at the moment.

"But I miss my friends! I miss my camp friends and

my Maryland friends," said Samantha. And that just made the waterworks start again.

"I know. I do too. But just think. When we get off the plane, Mama and Daddy will be there waiting. And we get to see our new house today. It's going to be a great adventure."

"Do you think Gracie can come and visit us next week?" Samantha asked.

I shrugged. "I don't know about next week. But you can definitely e-mail her, or I'll show you how to IM on the computer."

"I want a cell phone so I can text my friends," she announced.

"You'll have to ask Mama and Daddy about that," I said. "Anyway, there's lots of ways to keep in touch."

Samantha seemed to calm down a little bit. I looked out the window and thought about how crazy the next few days were going to be—unpacking from camp, getting my new room organized, and then helping with all the other moving stuff that needed to be done.

Not to mention the letters I still needed to write to my gold friends. And quite a few to my silver friends too.

Don't miss a single camper's story-here's a sneak peek at Jordan's, in *Summer Camp Secrets: Fearless*

Sunday, June 15

There was really no reason why I should be nervous, but I was. And whenever I got nervous, I always felt it in my stomach. I kept reminding myself that today should be no big deal.

Mama, Eric, Madison, and I were outside in the driveway, packing the car with all our camp stuff at the ridiculously early hour of six thirty a.m. Who knew that the sun would even be up this early? It was—barely. But the whole world was draped in a soft half-light that made everything seem slightly unreal.

All of a sudden, I felt that cold sweat I'd felt so many times before.

"I'll be back in a sec," I told them. Luckily, the garage door was open. I raced inside to the bathroom and stood there panting for a few seconds. My upper lip was all broken out in beads of sweat. I had to concentrate really hard to keep my breakfast inside my stomach where it belonged, but at the moment, my Cheerios and apple juice were trying to rebel against me.

I grabbed a washcloth off the rack and ran it under the cold water. While I was wiping my face with it, Mama called to me through the closed door. "Jordan, honey? Are you throwing up?"

Did she always have to know every single disgusting detail of my life? "No! I'm washing my face!"

After a couple of seconds, I actually felt better, and the sick feeling passed. But when I opened the door, Mama was standing there, holding up the little bottle of Dramamine. "Do you need to take one of these?"

I frowned at her. "I don't know. Do you think I should?"

"Well, you know how windy those roads get really close to camp."

I sighed. "Okay. Don't tell Madison I almost threw up, all right? Tell her I was washing my face." I had a dream. A simple dream. I wanted to keep my stomach issues from becoming the viral video of the week. Was that asking too much?

"Ah, honey!" Mama rubbed my back. "Don't get so

nervous! You're an old pro this year! It's not like last year. You've got a lot of friends at camp now. And Molly will be with you, and Madison. And of course Eda, but try not to bother her today, because you know how busy Opening Day is for her."

I took the pill Mama held out for me and swallowed it with a gulp of water. Having her tell me I shouldn't get nervous made me feel even worse.

She was right. This was going to be my *second* summer at Camp Pine Haven, so why was I on the verge of regurgitating?

Mama has always said I have a "nervous stomach" because it doesn't take much to make me regurgitate. Of all the words for throwing up—vomit, puke, barf, hurl—I liked *regurgitate* the best. It sounded more . . . medical.

"I'm not nervous. I'm just . . . stressed," I told Mama, looking at my fingernails so I wouldn't have to see her concerned look. "You know—making sure I packed everything, all this rushing around . . ."

Madison and I were going to camp for a whole month, so there were five thousand details I had to worry about. Anytime some major event was going on—when we were leaving for a trip, or if it was the first day of school—it was like you could *feel* the stress in the air, crackling like electricity. At least I could.

"Well, if you're feeling okay now, Eric and Madison are waiting for us."

When we went outside, Maddy was leaning against the car with this know-it-all look on her face. Not quite a smile, but almost.

The first thing she said was, "Did you throw up?"

"No." I brushed past her and climbed into the backseat.

"I swear, Jordan, you're the only one I know who gets carsick before you even leave the driveway." She scooted in next to me.

"I did not throw up! And excuse me for not being born perfect like *some* people." I stared out my window at the snowball bush by the driveway so I could avoid looking at her.

"You're excused!" She said it all perky. She was always in a good mood. I slightly hated her for that personality flaw.

Being too perky and perfect were just about the only personality flaws my sister had. She was sixteen, she made straight As, she was the star of her field hockey team, and about thirty-seven different boys were in love with her. And *nothing* made her nervous.

Perfection in older sisters has been known to cause

regurgitation issues in younger sisters. I was fairly sure that medical studies had proven that.

Maddy fished through her purse, pulled out a stick of gum, and offered it to me. I shook my head. She unwrapped it and shoved it under my nose, but I ignored her. The snowball bush had my undivided attention.

Eric and Mama were climbing into the front seat.

Eric turned the engine on and peeked at us in the rearview mirror. "Ready, ladies?" My stepfather was the sweetest guy in the world. It drove him slightly crazy living in a houseful of females, but he always put up with it.

"Ready!" yelled perky, perfect Madison. She'd given up trying to get me to take the gum and was chewing it herself. We started backing out of the driveway.

We didn't have far to go, just down the street to my best friend Molly's house. Molly threw open the front door and raced down her steps the second we pulled in the driveway.

"Finally! I didn't think you'd ever get here!" She had her sleeping bag under one arm and her pillow under the other. Her parents came out, carrying Molly's trunk by the handles.

"Think we'll get all this gear in?" asked Molly's father when Eric opened our already full trunk. The two of them shifted the duffels, trunks, and bags around while Molly gave her mother one last hug.

Molly squeezed in between me and Madison. Good. We needed a barrier between us. Too bad the Great Wall of China wouldn't fit in the backseat.

"How many times did you throw up this morning?" she whispered.

"Zero! And I slightly hate you for even bringing it up," I whispered back.

Molly laughed. "See, you're getting better. I'm glad you didn't get sick. I almost called you to ask."

In lots of ways, Molly and I are complete opposites. She has brown eyes and super-straight brown hair cut really short and parted in the middle. I have blue eyes, and my blond hair is past my shoulders, with a little bit of curl to it. She's short and stocky; I'm taller and slimmer.

The fathers were finished packing the trunk, so they slammed it closed, and Molly's parents leaned into the open car door and took another ten minutes saying good-bye. Finally we were ready to leave.

After he got in, Eric turned around in the front seat and smiled at all of us. "Next stop, Camp Pine Haven for Girls!" He was the only one in the car who hadn't made a comment about my regurgitation issue. I loved him for that.

We backed out of Molly's driveway and headed down the street. My stomach felt completely normal now. Hopefully, it wouldn't turn on me later. It's truly sad when you can't even trust your own organs, but my stomach has betrayed me many times. I've learned the hard way to be suspicious of it.

Mama glanced over her shoulder at me. "Feeling okay, honey?" she asked with her forehead crinkled up in worry lines. "We'll turn the air conditioner on and get some cool air blowing on you, all right?"

I leaned my head back against the seat and closed my eyes. "I'm *fine*."

I hated the way everyone had to pay so much attention to me. But that was partly my fault for being so abnormal. I have never been good at dealing with new experiences, and it had been a really big deal for me to go away to summer camp in the first place.

At least no one had said anything about the "major meltdown" summer. That was one of the worst experiences of my life.

Two years ago when I was ten, I was all set to go to camp for the first time. Eda Thompson, one of Mama's best friends, is the director of Pine Haven, so how could my mother have two daughters and not send them to her best friend's summer camp?

Madison had started going to camp when she was eight, and she loved everything about Pine Haven. So of course, everyone expected me to be just like Madison, but I didn't want to go when I was eight. Or nine.

Finally when I was ten, I felt this huge amount of pressure to go. I didn't want to, but I knew Mama, Madison, and Eda were all expecting me to go, and they all kept saying, "Just wait till you get there. You'll love it!"

But about fifty different things worried me. It was for a whole month, so I knew I'd be homesick, even with Maddy there and with Eda looking out for me. I'd be sleeping in a strange bed, away from home. I'd have to swim in a lake that was really deep with water that was dark green and you couldn't see the bottom of it. There would be all these strange girls I wouldn't know. Maybe my counselor would be really mean.

So about a week before camp started, I had a slight meltdown.

Actually, it was more like a major meltdown.

I started crying and I didn't stop. I cried for about two whole days. Major, major waterworks.

Everyone tried to comfort me in various ways that did absolutely no good at all. And yes, there were some regurgitation episodes. Eventually Mama said, "Fine, you don't have to go. You can stay home and miss out on all the fun."

So I stopped crying and immediately felt better, but I could tell she was majorly disappointed in me. Half of me felt so incredibly relieved that I didn't have to go to camp, but the other half felt like the biggest failure in the world.

So last summer when I was eleven, I knew I couldn't back out of it again. Luckily, Molly had moved to our neighborhood at the beginning of fifth grade and we got to be best, best friends. She wanted to go with me last year, and she was so excited that she made me feel a lot better about camp, but I was still nervous in the beginning.

Molly elbowed me and grinned. "Just think, tomorrow we'll actually be riding horses again! I can't wait to see Merlin. I wonder if he'll remember me."

Molly and I loved horseback riding more than any other activity at Pine Haven. Listening to her talk about horses made me excited. Camp really was fun, even if I did get nervous about the first day.

"I wonder if Amber will be in our cabin," said Molly.

"I don't know, but Eda promised she'd put you and me together."

I felt a sinking feeling inside me when I said that.

Eda probably thought I would have another meltdown if Molly wasn't right by my side. Once you've had one meltdown, people keep expecting you to have additional ones.

Mama was always telling people, "Jordan is a little more cautious than Madison. Jordan needs a little more encouragement than Madison does. Jordan is more sensitive than Madison."

Translation: Madison is perfectly normal. Then there's my abnormal daughter.

Last summer I had managed to get through the whole month of camp without having a meltdown. But like that was a big deal.

This summer I had to do more than just survive camp. Last year, the day we got home, I heard Mama on the phone to Daddy, giving him a report of how things went. They've been divorced since I was five, but they still get along really well.

"Jordan survived!" I heard her telling him. Her voice sounded so relieved. "Yes, she made it through the whole session. I honestly thought Eda was going to call me and say we'd have to come get her, but she made it! She survived! Maddy? Oh, well, you know how Madison loves camp. She thrived, just like she always does."

After I'd overheard that conversation, I went to my

room and locked the door. I cried for an hour. *Jordan survived; Madison thrived.* It was a horrible rhyme stuck in my head that kept repeating itself over and over and over.

This summer, I couldn't just survive.

This summer, I wanted it to be my turn to thrive.

FIVE GIRLS. ONE ACADEMY. AND SOME SERIOUS ATTITUDE.

CANTERWOOD CREST

by Jessica Burkhart

TAKE THE REINS
BOOK 1

CHASING BLUE
BOOK 2

BEHIND THE BIT
BOOK 3

TRIPLE FAULT
BOOK 4

BEST ENEMIES
BOOK 5

LITTLE WHITE LIES
BOOK 6

RIVAL REVENGE
BOOK 7

HOME SWEET DRAMA
BOOK 8

CITY SECRETS
BOOK 9

Don't forget to check out the website for downloadables, quizzes, author vlogs, and more!

www.canterwoodcrest.com

FROM ALADDIN M!X   PUBLISHED BY SIMON & SCHUSTER

She's a self-proclaimed dork. She
has the coolest pen ever. She keeps
a top-secret diary.
Read it if you dare.

By Rachel Renee Russell

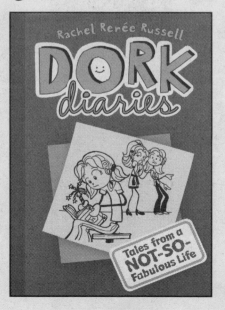

From Aladdin
Published by Simon & Schuster